Dear Reader,

The Coral Cove Series began with an invitation to join a group of fabulous authors in writing the "Stolen Hearts" novella series for Valentine's Day. Throughout the project, Coral Cove and its characters became family, and before *Heart's Desire* was complete, I knew Melanie and Sophie had amazing stories to tell as well. Since I adore the holidays, the "holiday" theme continued, and *Double Shot of Love* and *Mistletoe & Macaroons* were born. While I was writing the series, I began playing with recipes for the books and have included a recipe for a yummy creation at the end of each novella. Hope you enjoy both the stories and the confections!

Cadia

CADIA COX

THE CORAL COVE SERIES

HEART'S DESIRE
A Coral Cove Valentine Romance

DOUBLE SHOT OF LOVE
A Coral Cove Halloween Romance

MISTLETOE & MACAROONS
A Coral Cove Christmas Romance

Ten Story Books, LLC
Dallas, TX

THE CORAL COVE SERIES

ISBN-13: 978-1-945131-94-3
Copyright © 2017 Ten Story Books, LLC

The publisher acknowledges the copyright holder of the individual works as follows:

HEART'S DESIRE
Copyright © 2016 by Cadia Cox

DOUBLE SHOT OF LOVE
Copyright © 2016 by Cadia Cox

MISTLETOE & MACAROONS
Copyright © 2016 by Cadia Cox

Cover design by Ten Story Books, LLC
Cover photos: © BarbaraHelgason | Dreamstime.com
         © Rgb12 |Dreamstime.com   © Yarruta | Dreamstime.com
         © Jag_cz | iStockphoto.com   © fotojagodka | iStockphoto.com

Published by Ten Story Books, LLC
P.O. Box 701561, Dallas, TX 75370
Ten Story Books, LLC and the Ten Story Books logo are trademarks of Ten Story Books, LLC.

Please purchase only authorized editions.

For questions or more information, contact us at info@tenstorybooks.com.

CONTENTS

HEART'S DESIRE

A Coral Cove Valentine Romance

CADIA COX

Ten Story Books, LLC
Dallas, TX

To Eric,
my heart's desire

CHAPTER ONE

"That man's tongue should be illegal." Cassandra Baker slammed the phone onto the heart-shaped table beside her. "I haven't heard that much cursing since the Cowboys lost the playoffs." Jumping to her feet, she paced around Decadent Desserts, the business she started a year ago with her sister, Melanie. At twenty-four, the fraternal twins looked anything but related. Cassandra, older by two minutes, was tall and slender with blonde wavy hair, while Melanie was petite and curvy with auburn corkscrew curls. They assumed their mother must have been buxom because they shared that one voluptuous trait.

Cassandra's Sperry Top-Siders squeaked on the black-and-white tile floor as she blew errant bangs away from her eyes and quickly completed another lap through the chocolate shop. She pulled her hair up into a loose ponytail as she walked, looping the long strands through the opening in the back of her ball cap. Furrowing her arched brows over her hazel eyes, she tried to conjure up a solution to her latest crisis. "Mel, you know I don't work well under stress. I need order. Organization. Shipments that arrive on time. We *have* to make this business a success."

Melanie withdrew a box containing the sure, if temporary, cure from the fridge. "Eat up, honey. At least you'll feel better for a minute."

Cassandra slowed long enough to nab a dark chocolate heart filled with toffee crumbles, infused with a touch of almond flavoring, and sprinkled with pink Himalayan salt. She slid it slowly onto her tongue. "Mmmmm." She hummed as her long lashes fluttered, then gently closed.

"'Heart's Desire' is such a great name for these puppies." Melanie congratulated herself. She popped a piece of Cassandra's signature chocolate creation into her mouth, adjusted her Texas Rangers ball cap, and propped her cowboy boots on the glass coffee table. "So what's up with our newest biggest client this morning?"

"He just doled out the tongue-lashing of the year." Cassandra waved her fingers—tipped with almost non-existent nails—as if willing the phone to spontaneously combust. She sketched a new zigzag path through the store, then caught her reflection in the glass door and stopped to inspect herself. "Look at me," she said. "I'm a complete mess." Her white tank top looked like an impressionistic painting, streaked with chocolate, butter, and remnants of homemade pink frosting. To complete her look, purple food coloring stained her cutoffs, flecks of fondant clung to her high cheekbones, and a dab of baking powder adorned her long Grecian nose.

Peering closer at her reflection in the glass, she pursed her full lips and let out a frustrated breath. "Of course. Why would anything go right today?" She removed her pink Coral Cove Cougars cap, courtesy of the middle school girls' softball team the store sponsored, and tried to wipe sticky caramel off the brim. "Good gracious, I have to fix this."

"Fix what?" Melanie said. "You're doing it again, going all internal. Just spit it out."

Cassandra picked up her pace, nearly knocking over pink boxes bound with ivory ribbon neatly stacked on the counter like the great pyramids of Egypt. She had finished the display moments before the phone had rung. "That—*beast*—in Arizona says he hasn't received the Heart's Desires."

"What do you mean he hasn't received them? Valentine's is tomorrow!" Melanie scraped a hand through her curls. "I sent them by overnight shipping. Cost us a bloody fortune with all the dry ice. Why would anyone ever have a business in the middle of the desert? Christ, even in February everything melts there."

Cassandra tossed her cap behind the counter, then pulled on her fingers while wearing out the little bit of tread left on her shoes. "The buffoon is bound and determined to have those chocolates as a Valentine's bonus for all his employees. And he said if I don't track down that shipment, I have to personally deliver a replacement. Or he'll sue me for breach of contract."

"Did you say sue?" Melanie went pale.

"That's right, little sister," Cassandra glowered. "If that happens, we can kiss Decadent Desserts good-bye."

***

Nicholas Sterling hated Valentine's Day. All the red roses and chocolate hearts cluttering up everyone's desks, endless love songs playing on the radio, and worst of all, the memory of Valentine's Day last year—walking in to find his girlfriend....

Nope. No more falling in love for him—ever again.

He slammed his cell phone down on the mahogany desk he had recently inherited along with that other little bequeathal: Sterling Industries. "Damn. I can't believe that ditz lost my chocolate." He ground his teeth and felt his muscles tensing beneath the tight black tee-shirt.

Dolores gently patted her son's strong wrist. "It'll all work out, Nicky. I have faith in Cassandra. And you have to stop lashing out with that wicked language. That sweet girl is probably shaking like a newborn kitten."

"I don't care about that contract-breaking excuse for a—"

Dolores gave him the same category of look he'd been on the receiving end of since uttering his first curse word at Thanksgiving dinner when he was eight. Almost twenty years of fighting to tame his words.

"Sorry, Mom." Nicholas took a deep breath and counted to thirteen. Ten never seemed to be enough. "I have so much on my plate right now. I just can't worry about this ridiculous idea of yours."

"But Nicky, dear, the Chocolate Bonus is a great idea. You have to realize most people love Valentine's Day. And your daddy, God rest his soul, always did something special for the employees on his favorite holiday. They work awfully hard to build the best homes west of the Mississippi. If Daddy were still here, he would be beaming at the thought of everyone sinking their teeth into Heart's Desires. I know I did the first time I experienced Cassandra's magnificent creation."

"You talk like she's your life-long bosom buddy. Hell, you've only met the girl once."

A gleam crossed Dolores' ice-blue eyes.

"I know, Mom. I know," Nicholas said, a grin emerging from one corner of his lips. "You always wanted a daughter. I still can't believe Dad's gone."

He stood to pace and ran a hand through whisky brown hair which desperately needed a trim to meet Air

Force regulations. With his six-foot-four solid frame, he felt like an imposter pacing around his late father's office.

"You've done a wonderful job keeping his company and his memory going, Nicky. I know you had to be on constant alert overseas, but I hope you can relax a little while you're here—you're more bark than bite, you know." She gave him a quick wink. "I know for a fact you wouldn't hurt a flea. And I realize you didn't want to leave the military for good and were getting ready to join the Reserves, but the timing was perfect. I'm so thankful you came home to take over, even if you are planning to return in a year."

Nicholas sat down next to his mother. The plush mauve cushion atop an oak settee was not as comfortable as it looked. He thought about his last assignment in Afghanistan, unrest bubbling under the surface. The adrenaline rush, the thrill of being in the middle of the action. He thrived on it. He missed it. Protecting his country and....

Shaking the memories away, he leaned over and took his mother's tiny porcelain hands in his massive tanned ones. He would move mountains for this woman. "I'll get you those chocolates." He squeezed a little. "If it's the last thing I do."

CHAPTER TWO

"What do you mean the chocolate is gone?" Cassandra put the phone in front of her mouth and yelled at the shipping company rep. Her toes curled. "Argh. Isn't there anything you can do?" She felt like cursing, but that would lower her to the level of the buffoon at Sterling. She forced herself to be calm. *Deep breath. Okay. Count: One...Two...Three....* "Please look into it and let me know what you find out."

She tucked the phone into the back pocket of her cutoffs, the ones that fit like a second skin with holes starting to appear from years of wear. "Well, there goes our business," she said, turning to face Melanie. "Straight down the tubes. Sayonara. I'm going to end up in the hoosegow." Her knees nearly buckled underneath her, fearing what would happen to Decadent Desserts if she couldn't recoup the losses.

Melanie rolled her emerald eyes. "Don't be so dramatic." She pulled a tray of cooled toffee bars from the refrigerator and fed them one by one into the food processor.

"The shipment seems to have *disappeared* somewhere between *hither and yon*," Cassandra said, using air quotes.

Melanie cocked her head and glanced around a stray curl flirting with her cheek.

"His exact words." Cassandra pinched her nose, trying to keep the tears at bay. "I don't understand how this could happen. I have the receipt right here."

Melanie turned the processor on to annihilate the crunchy bars into a fine powder. "Then I guess we better get this new batch ready for you to deliver." She yelled over the noisy machine.

"Are you crazy?" Cassandra shrieked. "Valentine's Day is tomorrow. This batch won't be ready until after the shipping office closes, and—" She checked her map app. "Arizona is at least a twenty-hour drive from here. And seriously, who names a town in the desert 'Shady Grove' anyway?"

Melanie lined up multiple red heart-shaped silicone molds on the granite work counter. "Hand me that box of ingredients, will ya?"

Cassandra crossed the store to accost the shipment that arrived two hours ago. "At least we have enough chocolate. Not that we'll make any money on this order now."

She withdrew several packages of dark chocolate chips, tossed them onto the hard counter, and began ripping open the containers.

"Easy. Easy with that stuff," Melanie said, grabbing for the ingredients. "Why don't you go run around the block or something? Don't take your frustration out on the merchandise." A grin slowly spread across her face, exposing a dimple. "I know what you need, Cass. You need a *man*."

"Oh please. I don't have time to schedule a haircut, much less go on a date." Cassandra unwrapped a package. "But you're right. Fuming won't solve the problem." She placed the chocolate chips in a double boiler to melt, then measured out her perfected amounts of pure butter, coconut oil, almond extract, and a dash of cayenne pepper for kick, all organic, of course. She lovingly stirred the melted confection and blended the remaining ingredients. Breathing in the spicy aroma, she laid down her purple spatula and stared into the bowl. The scent of warm chocolate calmed her when nothing else could. "There is no way we can get these to Sterling before the end of the day tomorrow. We're hosed. I'm going to have to return their money."

***

"You can't cancel my order!" Nicholas barked. "I don't care how far it is, I won't allow it. I want what I paid for. Why would I possibly care that the shipping company can't get it here on time? Drive the damn chocolate out

9

if you have to, but get it done. I expect it to arrive tomorrow—Valentine's Day—by five p.m. sharp."

"Patience, Nicky," Dolores whispered. "Put her on hold for a moment."

Nicholas shook his head. "Don't go away, Miss Baker," he said. "You hang up on me, and I'll put your company out of business." He pressed the mute button and turned to face his mother.

"Nicky, how dare you! What did they train you to be overseas—a tyrant? Gracious me." She clutched her chest and fanned herself with a sales brochure lying on the antique desk. "Your daddy is rolling over in his grave. Don't make that poor girl drive all the way from Texas to Arizona. Where are your manners? Why don't you send the company plane for her?"

"Are you out of your ever-fu...." A deep breath whooshed out of his lungs. "Sorry, Mom. Do you know how much that would cost the company? And for what? Some stinkin' chocolate?" He slammed his fist on the desk.

He'd been overreacting to everything after returning from the war, not able to find even an ounce of patience wedged between his anger and hot temper. *She's right—Howard probably is turning over in his grave, ashamed of what I've become.* Hell, even Nicholas was ashamed. When had he turned into such an ass? What had the war done to him? What would it take for him to become a good man again?

But still...the company plane? Not going to happen. "I won't do it."

"Yes, you will, Nicky, and you'll fly the plane yourself. With all that Air Force training, I assume you can fly a little jet."

"Of course I can fly the jet. I just don't want to."

Dolores narrowed her eyes and arched one brow. "What are we now, three?"

Nicholas started the trek toward thirteen in his head. *One...Two...Three.... Don't lose control. She's your mom. You wouldn't have anything if she and Howard hadn't taken you in.*

A smirk rippled his features. "Fine. I'll fly out as soon as the plane is ready and pick up your precious chocolate."

"You better be sure and bring the girl so it doesn't melt on the way. That would be awful. She knows how to treat it right."

"I am *not* flying with her. No way. Not in this lifetime."

Dolores gave him the signature look that said she wouldn't take no for an answer.

"Fine. But I'm shipping her back on a commercial flight."

CHAPTER THREE

Nicholas stretched his long legs, then strode down the stairs of the plane like a man on a mission. Detouring around a bank of storm clouds had taken an extra thirty-two minutes, so he was late. He hated being late. And the humidity. My Lord! How did anyone live in this sauna?

"Where is she?" He grumbled through a clenched jaw. Glancing over the wing, he squinted into the bright beams of the late afternoon sun. Marching past a small sign that read "Welcome to Coral Cove, Texas," he thrust open a glass door leading into the reception area of the small coastal terminal.

A couple of old veterans sat in plush leather chairs playing a lively game of checkers beside an ancient water cooler, while a brunette girl who couldn't have been a day over sixteen stood behind the desk in what clearly was her high school cheer uniform.

"You must be Mistuh Sterling," she said in a chipper voice. "That's a really cool plane ya have there." Smacking on a wad of gum, she stretched to see around him, extending her hand. "I'm Ashley. How fast does she go?"

"That's none of your business, young lady," Nicholas snapped. "Do you know where Cassandra Baker is? She was supposed to meet me at seven o'clock sharp. It's almost seven forty-five. She's late."

Ashley drew her face into a smirk and crossed her arms across her chest. "Maybe *she* was on time and left already, seeing as *you* are the one who's late. We may live way out in the country, but we got us these here things called watches." She tapped the silver dollar sized jewel circling her narrow wrist.

"Ash sure told him, didn't she, Ed?" One of the vets bobbed his white-haired head up and down like an ocean buoy in a summer storm.

"Sure did, Ralph," the bald vet chimed in. "They sure do raise belligerent boys these days. He needs to spend some time in the military. That'd straighten him out and get him some manners."

"Ain't that the truth," Ralph said, glancing over his bowed shoulder, then straining to lift out of his chair.

Nicholas stood tall and marched toward them. "I'll have you gentlemen know, I just returned from two tours in Afghanistan. United States Air Force."

"Don't act like it," Ed said, moving a black checker to an open spot on the board. "Sassin' our Ash and not even helpin' that poor girl out over there."

Nicholas turned to see Ralph waddling toward a floor-to-ceiling glass door that opened onto a portico at the other end of the terminal. With a grunt, he pushed it out a few inches so a disheveled girl could prop it open with a red and white cooler. *Scratch that*, Nicholas thought, feeling a thud deep in his chest. A disheveled angel. The late day sunrays reflected off her blonde hair which draped over a perfectly oval face that lit up when she hugged Ralph. Alluring arms flowed from an all-but-there white tank top, smeared with every color under the rainbow. She was either a kindergarten art teacher or a very messy baker.

Nicholas was drawn to her like he was drowning and she was his lifeline, but he couldn't get his legs to cooperate. Instead, he stood there with his mouth wide open, gaping at the goddess with sinfully long, slender legs that disappeared into the shortest Daisy Duke's he'd ever seen.

"You'll catch flies if you don't shut yer trap," Ed said. "Go help Ralph with that there door. He's got a bad heart."

"Yes, sir. Of course," Nicholas mumbled. He stumbled over the curled up edge of a rug and tumbled forward into the angel's arms. She smelled of vanilla and chocolate, and his breath hitched when her skin grazed his. Her soft hands reached up to grasp his arms, the touch sending an electric shock down his spine. She was

14

stronger than she looked, and he felt himself getting weaker by the second.

"Um, thanks," Nicholas said, trying to steady himself. He leaned down to pick up his pilot hat that had tumbled toward her feet.

"No problem," she said, tucking thick sections of hair behind her ears.

He extended his hand. "Nicholas Sterling."

The flames of hell couldn't have risen any faster than the color in her cheeks. "You? You're Mr. Sterling? I thought they were just sending a pilot."

"And you are...."

"Cassandra Baker, owner of Decadent Desserts. At least hopefully I'll still own the business after you sue me for whatever else you think I've done to sabotage your order."

He looked down at the string of coolers stretching end to end from the door all the way to a vintage army-green jeep double-parked by the curb. "Is *all* that mine?"

"It's all yours," Cassandra said. "Let's just get this loaded onto your plane and we'll be out of each other's hair forever."

Ralph dragged one of the coolers about a quarter of an inch, then another eighth. "Whatcha got in here, Cassidy? Gold bars?"

"Oh Ralph, please sit down. We don't want your heart to give out."

"That's right. Leave the heavy liftin' to us young'uns," Ed said, sliding another cooler a full inch before giving out of breath and lowering himself onto the lid.

"Here, I'll get that," Ashley said, positioning herself into a deep squat. "We had our weight-lifting class today and I dead-lifted twenty whole pounds." She won the distance contest at five-and-a-half inches before collapsing onto a cooler.

"Everybody just stop," Nicholas ordered, waving his arms and using his military voice.

"There's no need to be so ornery, young man," Ralph said. "We may not be as hoity-toity as you, but here we still got chivalry."

"The cavalry?" Ed said. "Where are they? Fetch me my gun!" He reached for his cane and pointed it at the cows lined up at the split-rail fence across the road.

"Hold on, sir," Nicholas said, helping Ed into a cowhide chair. "Now, everybody just stop what you're doing. I'll load the coolers onto the plane. I don't want to be responsible for any heart attacks."

Nicholas could have sworn he saw wings emerge behind Cassandra, but it had to have been a trick of the early evening light mixed with cottonwood swirling in the breeze. He shook his head and rolled up his sleeves. Looking directly into the depths of her hazel eyes, he felt he could lose himself in them. *Control yourself, there, buddy. She's the enemy, remember?*

"Here's the packing slip for your order," Cassandra said. "I threw in the coolers for free in the hopes you'll see fit not to ruin the business I've worked so hard to build. Please make sure they stay upright. I wouldn't want the chocolates to be marred during flight."

"You're right. That's why you're coming with me."

Cassandra stepped back and stumbled over Ralph, grabbing his shoulder. "You're kidding, right? There is no way on this planet I'm getting on *that* plane with you," she said, pointing toward the tarmac.

"That was the deal. I told you I expected *you* to deliver the chocolates. What if they start melting? Or worse, turn over? I refuse to explain to my mother why the chocolates arrived ruined."

"Your mother? What does she have to do with any of this?"

"Does the name 'Dolores' ring a bell?" Nicholas leaned forward and arched a brow, waiting for her to connect the dots.

Her eyes grew wide as understanding dawned. "You mean that nice, cultured, sophisticated, kind woman who visited my shop last week is *your* mother? How did she ever have a son turn out like *you?*" She slapped a hand over her mouth and her eyes went wide, realizing she actually said all that out loud.

Nicholas grunted and started counting to thirteen. "Yes, she *is* my mother, and I'm not very happy she found your shop. It's caused me every kind of grief. But getting back to business. You *are* flying back to Arizona with me. On this plane. With this chocolate. It has to arrive in perfect condition. Otherwise, as I said before, I'll see you in court."

"More likely it'll be in the morgue," she said, under her breath.

"What's that supposed to mean?" he said, glaring at her.

She squared her shoulders and looked him dead in the eye. "It means I'm terrified of flying."

Nicholas laughed out loud. "Surely you're joking. Haven't you ever flown before?" He watched Cassandra pull on her fingers as a look of fear—no, terror—filled her eyes. He softened slightly. "Look, I really need you to come. I promised my mother I'd bring you back with me. You know, to protect the chocolates?"

"I...I don't know." Panic took over residence in her worried eyes, but he thought he caught a glimmer of...hope?

"After we take off, you can come up and see the cockpit, and I'll explain what all the buttons and knobs are used for, how lift, flaps, and ailerons function, and when radio calls are made and to whom. I can teach you all about flying and how safe it is. Did you know there are five million car accidents per year with numerous fatalities as opposed to twenty or so flying accidents, most of which don't have any associated deaths? It's by far the safest way to travel." He reached for her trembling hands. "Starting your own business took courage, right? Flying is nothing compared to that. You'll be over your fear within the first half-hour—I promise."

***

Cassandra had never felt this sick in her life. Nausea always ruled her stomach when nerves met with excitement. *I have to get over this fear once and for all. If I don't, how will I ever taste éclair au chocolat in France, cremino in Italy, or chocolate bon-bons in Switzerland?* She looked to the pilot. He seemed so sure of himself. So confident. *Maybe he can help me. Maybe, just maybe, he can erase the memory of....* She cut off her thought as she pushed back years of unshed tears threatening to burst through her self-imposed barrier.

"I'll do it." She got the words out before she could lose her nerve.

Nicholas loaded the last cooler, then led her to a supple leather chair. She heard his breath catch as he hesitated before fastening the safety belt over her cutoffs, then watched him shuffle toward the cockpit.

She was captivated by rock solid biceps flexing beneath his unforgiving white short-sleeved shirt that hugged every muscle. His strong, tanned fingers turned knobs and flipped switches deftly and quickly. The competence of those fingers mesmerized her, and she felt her temperature rise. *Why is this turning me on? Remember, he's about to put you out of business.*

"You ready to go?" Nicholas asked, turning to look at her.

"Not really, but just do it," she said, catching a whiff of his cologne in the air. It hinted of...amaretto. The almond-flavored liqueur had been her favorite scent forever, but she shook her head at the thought. "The quicker we can get there, the sooner I can get back on solid ground and into a rental car."

"When we get to altitude, I'll set the auto-pilot, then we'll get to 'Flying 101.' You'll love it!" Nicholas turned back to flick several more buttons, looking as excited as a kid with a new toy.

"Mr. Sterling, are you a good pilot?" Cassandra asked, holding her stomach tightly, hoping to squelch the butterflies and adrenaline mixing like oil and water.

"I'm a damn good pilot." Nicholas's laugh made her insides tremble. He exuded so much self-confidence that she figured his testosterone must be off the charts. And his lack of fear...it drew her to him like a kid to a chocolate bar. He was all male, ready to take to the skies, and she was falling fast.

The engines whizzed and whirred like dueling high-pitched tornadoes. But peering out the porthole-shaped window, her reflection proved what she knew to be true: her fear had turned her white as a sheet.

As the plane sped down the combination runway/taxiway, she closed her eyes, dug her short nails into the leather armrests, and prayed. *Please let this work. Please let this work.*

The plane lifted. She glanced quickly at the cars driving along the coastline, shrinking to smaller and smaller sizes until they looked like a line of ants discovering a picnic. She saw the Gulf beaches dip underneath the wing, but the rising bile in her throat tasted rancid. Thoughts from the past—of the crash that killed her parents—thrust fear into every inch of her body. Hyperventilation and dizziness waged war with her. They won, as her world quickly faded to black.

CHAPTER FOUR

The plane shook like the San Andreas Fault during an earthquake. The scent of amaretto swirled just out of reach as an echoing voice circled close, veered away, then moved closer. Tinny. Then alternately booming.

"Miss Baker, wake up. Miss Baker! Cassandra! Please be alive!"

Cassandra couldn't open her eyes to save her life, but she felt her chin being lifted and a pinching sensation closing off her nose. Warm, perfectly formed lips touched hers—lingered—and she begged the universe to let her keep dreaming. "More," she mumbled, imagining a handsome pilot making love to her on the open plains of a remote desert under a blue moon. But reality came crashing to life as a breath invaded her mouth. A forceful cough prompted her eyes to jerk open, and the darkness lifted. She fought to focus on a pair of dark chocolate-brown eyes beneath sexy brows harshly drawn together.

"Are you okay?" Nicholas asked. "You scared the hell out of me." He took her gently into his arms and held her close.

"I think I'm going to be sick."

Nicholas made sure she was stable and grabbed a sack from the seatback across the aisle. "Here's a bag. Can you sit up?"

She nodded her head, landing her hair in a twisted mess.

Nicholas helped lift her into a sitting position.

Glancing at the dim light outside the window, she saw they weren't moving. "What happened? How did I get on the floor?" Her stomach clenched, and she felt heaves threatening to take over. "Did we *crash?*"

"Nope. Emergency landing."

She jerked around to face him. "What emergency?"

"You," Nicholas said. "I've heard of people passing out from a fear of flying, but I've never actually seen it in person. When I put the plane on auto-pilot and came back to start the flying lesson, I found you unconscious. I had to land because I thought something else might be wrong. Once we were on the ground, I got you on the floor so I could start CPR."

She leaned toward the window and peered outside. Nothing appeared to exist from the plane to the horizon except dirt and a few buttes in the distance. "Where's the runway?"

"It used to be under us, but it appears someone decided to dig it up and hasn't gotten around to repaving it, much less issuing a NOTAM to inform pilots of the renovation. We're about a hundred miles east of El Paso. I've radioed for a doctor. He should be here soon."

Cassandra felt her heart sink. "I really don't think I need a doctor. I told you—I'm just afraid of flying and passed out. That's all." Embarrassment enveloped her, then she had a horrible thought. "Oh! What about the chocolates? Did they survive the crash? I mean, landing?"

"Seriously?" Nicholas said. "You're worried about the chocolate? You just passed out, I made an emergency landing in a jet on a dirt strip, and all you can think about is the chocolate?"

"Well, that's the reason we're on this trip, isn't it?"

***

We're on this trip because I was an ass, and you wanted to prove something to yourself, Nicholas thought. He grasped her hand, and his pulse raced as he nervously stroked her smooth skin. *And I'm starting to think I'm the luckiest guy on earth.*

Nicholas's heart rate had set a new record when he realized this amazing woman hadn't been kidding. She truly was terrified of flying. Seeing her unconscious and unresponsive triggered something in him. Something he hadn't felt...ever.

He rose from his knees, straightened his slacks, and walked toward the galley to fetch her a bottle of water. He hadn't been this scared since Afghanistan. Why did he even care about this woman? She was a thorn in his side, and now his plane would have to be repaired and recertified before it was airworthy again. And that was going to cost a fortune. But it was nothing compared to what he would pay if he didn't get her out of his head. She was messing with his senses. No woman got inside his mind. No woman had ever terrified him—not until he saw Cassandra's angelic face looking almost lifeless. He ran his fingers through his hair and shook his head. *Get your game face on, dude. Get it together. She's just a woman.* But she was unlike any he'd ever met.

Returning to Cassandra's side, he unscrewed the cap and knelt beside her. "Do you think you can drink any of this?"

She reached for the bottle, then withdrew her hand and scrunched up her face. "Why are you suddenly being so nice?"

"You scared the shit out of me—pardon my French." His voice shook, and he clutched the bottle. "Look, I'm sorry I've been so ornery. I just got back to the States recently from my last tour overseas, and it's been...difficult...transitioning to civilian life. I know it's no excuse, but really, I'm a pretty nice guy. I just have to remember to get out of 'military mode.'" He thrust the drink toward her. "Please, drink the water."

She gripped the container and filled her mouth with liquid. Her neck arched as the crisp water slid down her throat, relieving the parched passageway. "That feels good," she said. She ran her tongue over her lips, trembling, pink, and full.

"Not half as good as it looks," he whispered. Nicholas wiped a spare drop from just underneath her lip and lingered there for longer than he anticipated. "Your skin. It feels so warm, so...." He drew his fingertip along the edge of her jaw, then along her cheek.

"I was worried," he whispered. "Must be...hell, I don't know. It's just...if I don't...." Her essence pulled him closer until his lips met hers again, but this time not for a lifesaving maneuver. Except he felt maybe it was for him. Being with her made him feel like he was regaining the humanity he lost in Afghanistan, becoming the man he knew he could be. Warmth ran through his veins as he sank deeper into the kiss. He felt her tense for a brief moment, then her muscles relaxed. She pulled him toward her, urging him on. Willingly, he went.

"Pardon me, but is *this* the emergency I got called back from my fishin' trip for?"

Nicholas jerked his head toward the intruding voice and cleared his throat. "Doctor Adams?"

"My patients call me 'Doc Adams,'" the elderly gentleman said. Amusement danced in his eyes as he removed a pair of round spectacles, wiping them on his plaid shirttail. "So what's the emergency?"

Nicholas rose to his feet and shook the doctor's hand. He pointed toward Cassandra like she was a prize on *The Price is Right*.

She gently touched her lips, then clasped her slim fingers in her lap.

"I'm Nicholas Sterling, sir, and our patient is Cassandra Baker. She passed out, stone cold, once we were airborne. I'm the only crew on board, and even though I have Air Force training, I'm not a doctor and was afraid it might be something else. I started CPR, then realized she was conscious."

"Mmm hmm. I see." The doctor lowered himself to the seat beside Cassandra, withdrew his stethoscope from a vintage black leather bag, and tucked the ends into his ears. He listened to her heart and lungs, then felt of her forehead, shined a light in her eyes, and peered down her throat. He grasped her wrist to check the pulse, then looked up at Nicholas with mock alarm. "A little high on the pulse."

Nicholas felt something in his face he had not felt in a long time: blush.

"But that's about it," the doctor said. "Looks like she simply passed out."

"Are you sure, sir?" Nicholas asked, worry etching his forehead. When had his heart beaten so furiously in his chest? Was he actually...afraid? Couldn't be. It had to be indigestion from the burrito he ate for lunch.

"Pretty sure," Doc Adams said. "I've been in this business sixty-five years. I can spot this sort of thing a mile away. Like how you two feel about each other. It's nice to see good old-fashioned love in the air these days." He chuckled at his pun.

Nicholas sputtered, and Cassandra choked on her swig of water.

"You two deny it all you want, but these eyes have seen it all," the doctor said, waving two fingers in front of his face. "Would you folks like a ride into town? It's past sundown, and thanks to this heat wave, it's gonna stay hot as Hades out here."

Nicholas looked at Cassandra who sat quietly in the seat across from him, then back at the doctor. "Yes, sir. Please. Is there a hotel there? A place we can rent a car?"

"A car?" Cassandra questioned.

The doctor scratched his gray whiskers and winked at them. "I think we can come up with something for you two love birds."

CHAPTER FIVE

"I didn't think these things ran anymore, Mr. Sterling," Cassandra said, leaning toward Nicholas in the back of the black Model T.

He laughed...deep, rich, and all male. "It's probably the same vintage as he is. But he's a sweet old coot." He grasped her hand and caressed it. "And please, call me Nicholas. Are you feeling better, Cassandra?" He wished she'd scoot closer to him so he could feel her warmth again.

Just then, as if she'd heard his innermost pleas, she leaned her head against him. It felt like heaven...for a moment. He could feel her looking up at him, felt the question in her tense shoulders.

"It's okay," he said. "Lean on me if it makes you feel better. You've had quite a day." He nestled her close, draping his arm around her, pulling her near. "I promise I won't bite."

She relaxed for a few moments, then shuddered and drew back. "Bite! What about the chocolate? It might melt out there!"

"Enough with the chocolate," he chuckled. "I'll rent a car in town and go get it. I think it survived the rough landing, but I'll go check it after you're settled into the hotel."

"Ain't a hotel," the doctor said, twisting back to talk to them. "It's a fancy Bed and Breakfast. My wife, Ethel, runs it. Only 'bout a population of two-hundred or so in Dry Creek, but we're a friendly lot."

Three miles later, across dry dirt roads traversed by an occasional tumbleweed, the doctor pulled into a gravel drive lined with pansies and forget-me-nots. A charming Victorian home complete with terraces and turrets sat on a slight hill just past two rows of the flowers in full bloom. A hand-painted sign that read "The Botanical B&B" stood to the left of a narrow path leading to the house. A short woman with a welcoming smile and silver hair pulled back into a small bun stood on the top step, running her hands down a short green and yellow paisley apron.

"Ethel, this here's Nicholas and Cassandra. She passed out mid-flight, and he landed to get her some doctorin'."

"How sweet, dear," Ethel said, placing her hand over her heart. "Chivalry lives on, indeed." She motioned for her guests to climb the stairs. "I have a room ready for y'all, and Doc says you'll need a car." She pointed to a late model midnight blue SUV. "Maybelle's all yours as long as you need her. Our boy, Jeffrey, sent her to us for our fiftieth wedding anniversary. She hasn't got many miles on her, but she sure has lots of room for spreading out."

"That's very generous of you, ma'am," Nicholas said. "Thank you very much."

He squeezed Cassandra's hand and led her up the stairs. Turning to her, he said, "No more flying for you. We're driving the rest of the way."

She stopped mid-stride and faced him. "Why *are* you being nice to me? You were ready to see me in court less than two hours ago."

Nicholas looked off to a far horizon. "Something changed my mind."

That "something," of course, was her.

***

Cassandra frowned and slowly turned around the violet-themed room. Potted violets lined the windowsill, and someone had hand-painted a border of the purple flowers just under the dated crown molding. A lavender crochet blanket draped across a puffy sofa that sat beside an antique sewing table. "They really only have the one room?"

"I'm afraid so," Nicholas said. "And there's only one bed in here. When they said Bed and Breakfast, I guess they really meant it. A Bed." He gestured to the quilt-covered rectangle, more a nest than a bed.

"Wonder who gets the Breakfast." Cassandra smirked.

"Look, I'll go sleep in the SUV," Nicholas assured her. "Or I might just bed down in the plane. I need to go load up the chocolate anyway and make sure there's still some dry ice."

Cassandra glanced at the bed again.

Nicholas placed his hands gently on her shoulders. "Are you sure you're okay?"

She shivered at his touch. *I'm not sure at all. You make me feel things I've never felt before. All I want is to touch you—explore you—and to have you touch me. But I can't give in...I just can't. Melanie needs me, and the business depends on me. All a man will do is get in the way of my plans.* "I'm sure," she whispered.

"Goodnight, then," Nicholas said. Silence hung between them like the heavy air before a summer storm. Nicholas reached for the doorknob—

"You can sleep on the sofa. If you want."

He glanced toward the vintage piece of furniture. "Thanks for the offer. It looks more comfortable than the other options." He gave her shoulders a slight squeeze, then turned toward the door.

After Nicholas left the room, Cassandra let out the breath she didn't realize she was holding, dug her cell phone out of her bag, and dialed.

"Where the hell are you?" Melanie demanded. "Are you okay? When are you coming back to help me clean up this mess?"

Cassandra sank into the feather mattress and closed her eyes. "You won't believe what happened."

"Try me, then get your butt back here to help."

"As much as I hate that part of the business, I wish I could. But I'm stuck in west Texas."

"You're *where?*"

"In Dry Creek, a tiny dot on the map somewhere near El Paso."

"What the *hell* are you doing way out there?"

Cassandra told Melanie everything that had transpired, from the airport scene to the emergency landing to the B&B.

Melanie interrupted her. "You *flew?*"

"I know. Unbelievable, right?"

"More like life-altering. What was it like?"

"Ugh. I don't want to talk about it."

"Okay...so...how's the chocolate?" Melanie asked.

"I assume it's fine. Nicholas is on his way to check on it at the plane."

"Oh, so it's 'Nicholas' now. Something's different with you, Cass. It's in your voice. You're not telling me everything."

Cassandra's thoughts went to the kiss and the feel of Nicholas's lips moving over hers. She thought of how easily she could become addicted to the aroma of his almond-scented cologne and how arousing his laugh could be. Pushing the thoughts from her mind, she said, "There's nothing different."

"You *like* him, don't you? Well, glory be — Jesus is comin'! It's about time you started dating someone."

"I do like him, but not that way. I can't. I have a business to run. I have to make a success of it, and a man would only distract me from my goal."

"You sound like a robot, Cass," Melanie said. "Something about that man made you face your fear of flying. No one has ever had that kind of effect on you. Just remember, goals won't keep you warm at night."

So true. She'd had many a cold night lately. "But a padded bank account and a few years of retirement funds will make me sleep a whole lot better."

Silence took over the call.

"Mel? Are you there?"

"Yes, but obviously I haven't rubbed off on you one bit. You go after that man. You deserve happiness. Don't let this chance slip away."

"I'm just not ready yet," Cassandra said. *Maybe I never will be.* "My focus needs to be on the business."

"Touché." Melanie let out a sigh. "Alright, girl. Have sweet dreams. If they've got Nicholas in them, I'm sure they will be."

Cassandra heard a chuckle, then a click on the other end of the line. She hated to admit it, but she felt something when she was around Nicholas that she hadn't felt for years. Maybe not ever.

CHAPTER SIX

Nicholas tiptoed up the stairs, trying not to track dust all over Ethel and Doc Adams' home. He had inspected the grounded plane after securing the chocolate in the SUV and brought back the desert with him from head to toe.

He knocked gently above the bouquet of violets painted on the door. "It's Nicholas. May I come in?"

"Just a sec," Cassandra called.

He heard her shuffling toward him, then silence for a few seconds before the crystal doorknob magically turned to allow him entry.

"Hi," she whispered, poking her head around from behind the door.

Nicholas took a deep breath and stepped into the flower-themed room.

"Oh! Stay right there," she said, reaching a hand out to stop him. "You're a mess. I've never seen so much dust. You've got to get out of those clothes before this place starts to look like the desert. Stay here. Let me get some towels." She turned and scurried toward their tiny bathroom.

His breath caught as he saw her hair pinned up, exposing her bare back, not to mention the long legs emerging from a very small white towel wrapped around her slender body.

He stood, unable to move as he clenched his teeth and felt his pants shrink a size.

"Here you go," she said, jogging back toward him, holding out one towel and clasping hers close to her ample chest.

"God, you're beautiful." Nicholas saw a blush bloom in her cheeks as a soft smile emerged. He reached for the towel to keep from reaching for her. He tried to utter a coherent sentence, but she had taken his breath away.

The towel slipped out of his hand, and they knelt to grab it at the same time. His rough hand landed on top of hers, and a shiver ran down his spine. Lifting only his head, he looked into her freshly washed face and couldn't help himself.

Leaning forward, he placed his hand under her chin and lifted it slightly, lightly placing his lips on hers. Gently at first, until he heard her whimper and felt her weave a hand into his hair. He ran his fingers along her bare shoulders en route to removing a clip that kept her hair bunched in a messy ponytail. Lust caught in his throat as tendrils fell around her shoulders, covering his fingers.

Her moan undid him, and he crawled forward a couple of feet on the purple carpet and kicked the door shut with a dusty shoe.

***

The latch clicked as she clung to his kiss. *Oh God, he tastes of salt and...amaretto.* His scent enveloped her like a warm summer rain...sprinkled with fairy dust.

"There's something about a man in uniform," Cassandra whispered, nipping at his bottom lip. She felt her willpower dissipate, then evaporate. A surge of feminine power, of confidence, stepped into its place and invaded her fingertips as she began unbuttoning his shirt.

"And something about him being out of it." She never did anything like this. The first time she was with a man, he took control of everything and left her lacking. She assumed it was always like that and never took the lead. Not until tonight. Not until she kissed Nicholas. She felt her resolve crumble and decided maybe, just maybe, she could give in. Just this once.

Freeing him of his dusty shirt, she deftly turned the fabric in on itself so the dust was contained, and laid it on the towel she had brought for him. Breaking the kiss was the hardest thing she thought she'd ever done, but she wanted to see him—needed to see him. Sitting back on her knees, she slowly lowered her towel to the floor.

"Oh, good God in Heaven," Nicholas whispered, reaching out to caress every inch of her exposed skin.

She raised her eyes to take in his form, then reached out and stroked her fingers over solid abs dusted with the softest hair she had ever felt. She followed his treasure trail lightly with a fingertip until she felt it meet the cool metal of his belt.

He reached for his zipper, but she nudged his hand away.

"You've had so much to be in charge of in your life, Nicholas," she said. "Let me help relieve you of duty."

He gave in to her request.

***

Nicholas shuddered and clenched his fists by his side. He watched her face as she focused on his body. Took in every touch. Memorized every movement. He didn't dare move, fearing it might break the spell.

His zipper cried out in the quiet room, and he lifted up to give Cassandra better access. Every nerve in his body was on full alert. He wanted to leap forward, to take her right there on the faded purple carpet. But he gathered some strength, pulled from the deepest corners of his control, and let her take the lead. Maybe she could take away some of the pressure of his military years. Maybe, just maybe, she could help him transition back into being a man.

His eyes fluttered shut as her lips headed south. *Lord Jesus, just take me now.* He nearly died when she....

A knock sounded above them.

"Yoo-hoo!" Ethel's voice echoed on the other side of the door.

Cassandra withdrew her hand as though she had touched a hot stove. Her eyes grew large, and her cheeks flamed red. She looked at what they weren't wearing and grabbed her towel from the floor. Quickly cinching it around her, she sprinted for the bathroom.

Nicholas tucked himself back into his pants as fast as humanly possible, zipped up and slowly opened the door a few inches.

"I have a nightgown and pj's for y'all to borrow," Ethel said, handing him the clean sleepwear. "Sleep as long as you like. I'll fix breakfast when I hear the water running. Sweet dreams, you two," she said with a wink and a quick wave.

Nicholas watched her scuttle down the hallway, then he shut the door and leaned against it. Fingering the nightclothes, he looked upward and cursed. "Can't a guy get a break?"

Walking to the bathroom, he gave a quick knock.

"Just hand me the gown, please," Cassandra said, opening the door a mere crack. "I'll be done in a second and you can have the bathroom."

"Cassandra—"

"Please don't say anything. We have to forget that happened. God, I'm so embarrassed."

"There's no need to be embarrassed. We—"

The door shut on him, and he heard the tap running over what might have been a series of groans.

Nicholas waited his turn, determined to talk to her after he changed, but she was sound asleep when he emerged from the tiny bathroom. He lay down on the sofa, tossing the blanket aside. But he did everything but sleep, reliving every touch, every kiss. Each time she made a noise or turned over, he woke to check on her. She slept fitfully, but he found he enjoyed watching over her. How she could look so sexy sprawled out on the bed in the granny gown amazed him. She was beautiful, sleeping with beams of moonlight draped over her like a silk bedsheet. The longer he studied her form, the harder he got. Knowing he couldn't do a thing about it, he rose with the sun and took an ice-cold shower.

CHAPTER SEVEN

Nicholas could tell the drive through the desert fascinated Cassandra. She asked questions about the cactus, mesquite trees, and why the creosote bushes were so evenly spaced in the dirt. He had spent his whole life in the desert, both at home and overseas. Funny, since he'd met Cassandra, he hadn't even thought about joining the Reserves. Had that really only been yesterday? He felt he'd known her forever. Watching her discover saguaros, prickly pears, and other cactus varieties unique to the desert landscape, he felt happier than he had in years. And oddly—peaceful.

"Do we have time to stop for a few minutes?" she asked.

"Sure. What's up?"

"I'd like to climb that butte over there. I've seen pictures, but never anything like this in real life. The rocks are so beautiful, so stately. That one doesn't look too tall, and I'd love to see what the desert looks like from up there."

"Your wish is my command," he said, excited to show her the area, thinking maybe she'd like it enough to want to stay in Arizona. *Whoa boy. Where did that come from?*

He shivered as he recalled why dating her was a bad idea, why he hated Valentine's Day in the first place. The image he'd tried to repress for a long, celibate year roared out of the depths of his memories. Last Valentine's Day—when he decided he would never fall in love again. *Think of something else, you moron.*

The SUV sunk a bit as he parked at the edge of a dirt trail. "We need to carry some water with us."

"But it's only a short hike." She hopped out, digging her heels into the rust-colored dirt. "We won't really need any."

Nicholas reached into the bag of supplies Ethel had packed for them. "This is the desert, Cassandra. No water, no climbing."

"Fine," she huffed. "Hand me a bottle." She grabbed it and started up the hill.

"Wait for me," Nicholas said, stuffing several bottles into his pants pockets.

They hiked in silence for twenty minutes, dodging prickly pears and jumping chollas before he couldn't take it any longer. "What's eating you?"

She stopped and turned. "You're treating me like a child. I'm a grown woman."

"You're a grown woman who hasn't ever lived in the desert. Do you know what dehydration can do to you? It's a lot worse than what heat does to chocolate."

Cassandra groaned, turned, and continued walking in silence. She hesitated a moment, then took a swig of water, leaning her head back and giving him a bird's eye view of her generous breasts stretched across the crisp white tank top, courtesy of a good washing by Ethel.

Nicholas enjoyed the view from where he was. Why did she have such a mesmerizing effect on him? He typically went for the beauty found in glossy magazines. Hers was the natural kind: easy and...perfect. And she seemed to hold her own, running her business and focusing on its success. Why did that turn him on just as much as her perfect body? And then there was her smile. He could live on the receiving end of that for a lifetime.

A rattling sound tore through his thoughts, and his muscles tensed. "Don't move, Cassandra."

She stopped mid-stride. "Is that what I think it is?" she whispered.

"Afraid so. The rattlesnake is under the bush behind you. Whatever you do, don't move."

"Snakes come in second only to planes," she said, visibly shaking. "Just so you know."

"Please don't pass out on me again." Reaching for a stick by his ankle, he slowly rose to his feet. The tan and brown snake raised its head and slithered beneath the bush, continuing its warning siren.

"Okay, now slowly walk forward, and I mean *slowly*."

She moved about an inch per shuffle.

He knew well how a rattler could strike out about half its length, and judging from the size of this guy, she needed another two feet or so of clearance. "Keep going, but slowly."

"Can't you throw a knife at it or something?" she whispered.

"There's an old saying, 'Nothing's worse than a cut snake.' I've heard their venom gets even more concentrated when they're wounded."

"Wonderful," Cassandra said. "I'm never leaving Coral Cove ever again."

Nicholas's heart sank at the thought of not seeing her once she returned home. But first things first. He had to get her out of harm's way. "Just a few more inches. You're doing great." He walked slowly to a rock about three feet in front of her, checking to make sure no scaly visitors were hiding out there.

"A couple more steps and you should be clear."

He opened his arms, and she fell into them. Her tears undid him as he wrapped her in his embrace. When he opened his eyes, he saw the rattler slithering to a more remote bush.

"You're safe now." Nicholas drew her near, cradling her head in his warm hand. He knew at that moment he would protect this woman at all costs. He never wanted to let her go.

She collapsed against him and broke into sobs. "This is the trip from hell."

His heart fell to his feet. Hearing her summary of the past day was like an ice pick to the chest because he couldn't help thinking the trip was one of the best he'd been on in years, if not ever. Spending time with this quirky, determined woman made him feel alive for the first time in ages. He hugged her close, taking the opportunity to rub circles on her back, his fingers grazing the skin at her waist. The breath caught in his throat.

She let out what sounded like a purr, held his face in her hands, and raised her lips to his. He knew the response came with the adrenaline rush from the encounter with the snake, but he welcomed it just the same. He dared to move his hands higher under her shirt, to feel more of what he craved from last night.

"Howdy, fellow hikers." A teenage boy smiled down from a rock formation above them. He shoved a pair of Coke-bottle glasses up closer to his eyes and shifted his backpack that looked outfitted for at least a two-week journey. "Seen anything interesting up here?"

Nicholas threw a glance toward the sky. *Seriously? Is one break too much to ask for?* He stepped back from Cassandra and sneered at the hiker.

Cassandra smoothed her shirt down and took a drink of water. "Too much for me. I think I'm ready to go. Nicholas, would you please lead the way?"

He knew she meant down the butte, but he wished she meant exploring the path both their hearts seemed to have chosen.

***

At each stop along the highway, Cassandra checked on the chocolates. So far, only one box had been affected.

"Mom was right," Nicholas said. "These things are magnificent."

Cassandra reached over and grabbed a Heart's Desire. Warmth invaded her belly and pride blossomed in her heart as she fed Nicholas the chocolates one by one. These were her chocolates. Her creations. A taste of her....

He took her hand in his and planted a gentle kiss on it. "You are an amazing woman, Cassandra Baker. Don't you ever forget that."

His seductive grin melted her resolve. She couldn't get the feel of his hands and lips out of her mind.

"So...are you dating anyone?" Nicholas asked.

She pursed her lips and cocked her head. "Actually, I'm married."

His heart pounded against his chest, and he felt hyperventilation threatening. He swerved and barely missed ramming an eighteen-wheeler.

Cassandra screamed as she dug her nails into the armrests. "Married to Decadent Desserts! Geez, do you think I would kiss you and almost—you know—if I were dating someone? Or Heaven forbid—*married*?!"

Nicholas pulled the SUV to the shoulder, shifted into park, and laid his head on the smooth wood of the steering wheel. He shrugged his shoulders. "I've been on the wrong end of that game before. Thought I should ask."

"What happened?" she asked quietly, not at all sure she wanted to hear it.

CHAPTER EIGHT

Nicholas couldn't tell her what happened. Hell, he'd only known her one day. How could he trust her with his secret? With his pain? He'd never shared with anyone the details of his devastating breakup. Why did he feel like he wanted to tell her, needed to tell her? He stared into the distance and took a deep breath.

"It was my first day back stateside in a year—last Valentine's Day, in fact. I was going to surprise my girlfriend. But seems the person I surprised most was the man lying underneath her...in *my* bed." Nicholas was quiet for a while, shivering at the memory. "We'd dated for three years. She said she couldn't take going to bed alone anymore while I was deployed. I stopped myself before I did anything I'd regret, left the house, and proceeded to get the drunkest I've ever been. And I caught the next flight back overseas."

He looked up at Cassandra, wondering why he had dared share the hurt, the embarrassment, the betrayal with this woman. "I've never told the details of what happened to anyone. I just walked out of there and decided to never fall in love again. I—" He took a deep breath and held it in. When he finally let it go, he felt a bit of the pain leave with it. He looked into her eyes and realized it felt—cleansing—to bear his soul to Cassandra. "I couldn't handle getting my heart broken again."

Cassandra gently put her hand over his. He could feel her warmth healing the wound. Strange.

"But something about being with you makes me question that decision," he whispered. "When I kiss you, feel your touch, it's like the planets are all aligned for the first time in...forever."

"Nicholas," she said, squeezing his hand tightly.

He felt the impulse, as though she were healing his heart. And words evaded him.

"You've awakened something in me, too," Cassandra said. "I feel...alive, adventurous, daring, ready to take on the world. I mean, you actually got me on an airplane." She gripped his hand. "And...it scares me." She glanced out the window, then looked back into his eyes. "But I'm sorry. I have to keep my focus on my business."

When she withdrew her hand, he felt alone. Empty.

Silence filled the SUV. After Nicholas mentally withdrew the emotional dagger she'd twisted and thrust into his heart, he did his best to appear unshaken and pulled back onto the highway. He stared into the distance as the miles passed, along with chollas and desert rock formations.

The concrete road against the tires made a clunking sound as they passed through Tucson and headed north.

Finally, Cassandra broke the uneasy quietness. "What does Sterling Industries do?"

"We build homes," Nicholas said. "That's been the focus ever since my granddad started the business in the fifties. Back then, Phoenix had just started sprouting as a city. My dad took over in the late eighties, right after he and Mom settled just north of town in Shady Grove. Then they adopted me."

"Adopted?" Cassandra turned to look at him. "How old were you?"

"I was eight...and a hellion. I'd run away from one too many foster homes when I started sleeping in houses that were under construction." Lost in the memories, he chuckled. "I got away with it, too, until Howard—my adopted dad—got suspicious about all the odd food wrappers his morning crews kept finding. I did a lot of dumpster-diving back then to find something to eat. But it all worked out in the end. The day he found me, Howard took me home to one of Dolores's home-cooked meals, and she refused to let me leave. It was warm there...and full of love. And I never went hungry. I was smart enough not to look a gift-horse in the mouth, so I cleaned up my act and was on my best behavior from that day forward. They gave me so much. I wanted to do something to repay them, so I decided it was my life-goal to protect them. To keep them safe. I chose the career I thought would best accomplish that: the military. And I found a second family there."

***

Cassandra was quiet for a few moments, then cleared her throat. She ached for the boy he had been, understood why he told her his secrets. Blinking back tears, she knew it was time to tell him hers.

"I don't remember much about my real parents, either. They died in...a plane crash."

"Oh, I'm so—"

She held up a hand and interrupted him, needing to tell him everything. "My sister and I found out about the accident when Child Protective Services showed up at our kindergarten and took Melanie and me to our first foster home."

"Cassandra, I'm so sorry." Nicholas turned to look at her, empathy filling his gaze. He reached for her, hating the emptiness he felt. "Oh my God. That's why you're terrified of planes."

"According to my therapist, it is. Neither Melanie nor I have ever been on one...until yesterday."

Nicholas shook his head, his white knuckles gripping the steering wheel. "I can't tell you how sorry I am for talking you into getting on that plane."

"It's okay," she said. "I've wanted to get over my fear of flying for years. There are so many places I want to visit, so many countries and cultures I want to experience. I honestly thought you might be the one to cure me. Anyway, Melanie and the business are all I have. Our foster family wouldn't allow us to go back into our house. They said we needed to make new memories...make a new life."

She wiped a tear from the corner of her eye. "I don't even have a photo of my real parents." She looked out the window and regained her composure. "Our last foster family paid for one year of college for both of us. The rest was covered by student loans and odd jobs. We agreed that we'd invest every dime of our small inheritance in the business we dreamed of starting together. I'm assuming either my mom or dad was good in the kitchen. At least I like to think I got my knack for creating confections from one of them. I have to make Decadent Desserts a success. I just have to. I'd love to expand, but right now, I simply can't afford it. It's all I can do to pay rent on the shop space we have."

"I could give you a loan if you need one," Nicholas said. In one breath it hit him like a blow to the chest:

he'd do anything to protect this self-reliant, determined woman that had hijacked his heart.

She placed her hand over the one he extended toward her. "Thanks for the offer, but I'm holding things together. You are actually my biggest client, so as long as I keep you happy, Decadent Desserts is safe...for the time being."

CHAPTER NINE

The SUV pulled up to Sterling Industries at five o'clock on the dot. Nicholas had the receptionist make a company-wide announcement, asking all the employees to meet in the lobby. He handed Cassandra the keys so he could unload the coolers.

Cassandra slid the keys into her pocket and began stacking the pink heart-shaped boxes, creating three large, perfectly symmetrical pyramids around the room. Proud of their accomplishment, she and Nicholas stood hand in hand.

Dolores met them with a smile and a microphone. "I'm so thrilled you're here, Cassandra. It's good to see you again. I hear you've had quite an adventurous couple of days."

"How did she know what happened?" Cassandra whispered to Nicholas. He shrugged his shoulders.

"It's good to see you again, Dolores." She smiled as Nicholas's mother wrapped her in a hug. It felt warm and welcoming, like...home.

Nicholas cleared his throat and raised the microphone. "Good afternoon, everyone. On behalf of my mother, and in memory of Howard, this year we are continuing his tradition of a Chocolate Bonus for Valentine's Day: his favorite holiday."

A tear crept down Dolores's cheek as she beamed at Nicholas.

"As many of you know, Dolores was in Coral Cove last week. During her time there, she visited Decadent Desserts, the brainchild of chocolatier Cassandra Baker." He extended his arm toward Cassandra who took a quick bow. "There, she uncovered some of the world's finest chocolates."

Cassandra had never felt so proud, hearing these words from Nicholas. Her heart swelled with love. So much so, she thought it would burst from happiness.

"So, in honor of Valentine's Day, Sterling Industries would like to present each one of our employees—no, our partners—with a box of Heart's Desires, Cassandra's signature creation. We couldn't have the success we do without each and every one of you. Dolores, Cassandra, and I will be passing out the boxes at the pyramids around the room. Happy Valentine's Day to you all!"

Nicholas squeezed Cassandra's hand and walked her to the closest pyramid. "Happy Valentine's Day, Cassandra." He gave her a brief kiss, followed by hoots and hollers from their audience. "Do you mind handing these out?"

"Not at all!" She beamed with pride.

Foremen, carpenters, receptionists, salespeople, and office staff lined up to receive their chocolates. The two-story glass atrium echoed laughter and oooh's and aaah's over the delicious confections. A dozen questions greeted Cassandra: How did you make it so creamy? What gives it that extra kick? Can I order more online?

Her business was about to explode, thanks to Nicolas Sterling. She locked her eyes with his over the crowd, and they shared a smile.

Over the next twenty minutes, she handed out box after box until there were more people in her line than there were boxes left. A glance at the other tables told her Nicholas had miscalculated. Soon, he was the only one left with boxes and a long line of employees.

"Dolores," Cassandra whispered. "What are we going to do? Nicholas obviously didn't order enough."

Laying cool fingers atop Cassandra's shoulder, Dolores said, "Don't worry, dear. I think everything will work out just fine."

Dolores's heels clicked across the marble floor as she approached a solid walnut door by the entryway. Pushing down on the handle, the door cracked open and Cassandra saw....

No! It can't be! A room full of pink boxes of Heart's Desires, hidden behind the door, complete with their ivory ribbons.

"Over here, everyone!" Dolores shouted. "We have more!"

Cassandra's heart sank as the realization struck: Nicholas had lied to her. He'd had the original shipment all along.

***

Tears stung her face as Cassandra fled the building and flung herself into the SUV. She dropped the keys as she fumbled to push them into the ignition. After wiping her eyes, she focused on the steering column, and the key slid in. She revved the engine as Nicholas banged on the passenger-side window, screaming her name.

A heavy sob escaped her lungs as she shook her head, no longer able to look at him. She slid the gearshift into drive and sped out of the parking lot. Catching his reflection in the rearview mirror, she turned her eyes from the man who had stolen not only her chocolates but also her heart.

CHAPTER TEN

Cassandra wiped beads of sweat from her brow as she finished hand-mixing the batter for a new creation she'd been working on. The fan blades overhead beat the humid air, slapping at it like beater blades whipping up merengue.

Ralph and Ed sat in two oversized red leather chairs separated by a glass coffee table and their game of checkers.

"Sure is toasty today," Ralph said, moving a red checker to an open space on the board. "You ready for us to be taste-testers yet, Cassidy?"

"Hold your horses, Ralph," Ed said. "She'll let us know when she's ready for our services." He saluted and winked at her.

Cassandra withdrew two demitasse spoons from the silverware drawer, dipped them into the batter, and walked toward her honorary taste-testers.

Ralph looked over the spoon from every angle, swirled it under his nose, inhaled the rich aroma, then stuck out his tongue to dab a touch of the batter onto it.

Ed reached over and shoved the spoon into Ralph's mouth. "Ya can't taste it if ya don't put the whole thing in yer trap." Licking the remnants from his own spoon, he closed his eyes and smiled toward the heavens. "Cassidy, you've outdone yourself. This here's sinful stuff."

Cassandra grinned for the first time since returning from Arizona.

"Yay! Success!" Melanie pumped a fist into the air above her. "Why don't you take some time off now, sis? I can hold down the fort here."

Cassandra took a spoon from the drawer and gathered a small dollop of batter to taste. "No way. I've got to get our revenues back on track after the fiasco last month. I think this needs a little more amaretto flavor." She dug into the cupboard and withdrew a new bottle of almond extract.

"I really think you should take a break," Melanie said. "Why don't you go home, take a shower, and put on one of those cute little sun dresses. It'll make you feel better."

"Mel, let it go. I'm not going to dress up. I'm going to work. I need to get ahead this month, and a new recipe is the way to do it. I have to cover the losses, so let it go."

"Yeah," Ed said. "Let her work, Mel. We need to do more tastin' just to make sure it's right."

Ralph reclined in his chair. "Any more tastin' and that big belly of yours won't be able to stay in your britches."

"I keep telling you everything will work out," Melanie said. "I'm sure of it. I don't know why you won't believe me." She smirked and rolled her eyes. "Look, I'm heading to the grocery store for a few supplies. At least put on some lipstick."

Cassandra threw a dollop of batter at her sister. "Get out of here, you crazy thing. Why do you care so much about how I look today? Geez." She flipped her hand in the air toward the door. "Go on. Get out of here."

"Fine! I'm going! I'm going!" Melanie withdrew a tube of Passion Pink lipstick from her purse and tossed it to Cassandra. "Put some on, sis." The bell over the door tinkled as she walked out of the store.

Cassandra rolled her eyes, tossed the lipstick tube behind a box of dark chocolate sea salt caramels, then returned to her latest project.

Deep in thought, she sat to calculate measurements for the new recipe. Doodles covered the page with possible names: Amaretto Surprise, Almond Delight, Essence of Nicholas.

The bell tinkled again, but Cassandra didn't look up. If Melanie needed something, she could grab it herself.

"Uh-oh," Ralph whispered to Ed. "Here comes trouble."

"Essence of Nicholas?" a deep voice said. "I kind of like the sound of that one."

Cassandra's head jerked up to see the face she hadn't been able to banish from her memory for three weeks, six days, and seven hours. Excitement coursed through her veins as she instinctively rose to move toward him. The feeling lasted for all of two-and-a-half seconds until the memory of discovering the chocolates in the storeroom came flooding back, and she collapsed into the chair.

"Cassandra, please, just hear me out."

"How dare you come here, to my place of business, after you...you...." She sprang to her feet and started pacing the room in a figure eight. Stopping with her back to the door, she glared at him, yet felt like a deflated balloon. "You lied to me."

Melanie blew back in the door. "Sis, you've gotta see this super-cool Caddy outside! It's awesome! So vintage!"

"Not now, Mel," Ed said. "The show's just startin'."

"But...." Melanie's eyes grew large as she saw the sexy man standing near the chocolate counter.

"I think I'll be leaving now," Melanie said, backing toward the door.

"Oh no you don't." Nicholas curved a finger and motioned for her to come back.

"You can't order my sister around, *Mister* Sterling," Cassandra snapped.

"Yeah," Ralph and Ed said in unison, trying to extract themselves from the cushy chairs.

"You git out, mister!" Ed snapped. "You made our Cassidy cry."

"That's right," Ralph sputtered. "And you say you're military. Hogwash. We don't treat our ladies like that. Only real gentlemen are welcome here. Now git. You can't talk to her like that." Ralph swooshed both hands toward the door, making himself so unbalanced he fell back into his chair.

"Oh yes I can, sir," Nicholas said. "Especially when my trip here involves both of these ladies." He walked toward Cassandra. "Please sit down, both of you."

"Okay," Melanie said quickly, sliding into a chair at the nearest table.

Cassandra continued pacing the floor.

"She does that when she's nervous," Melanie whispered to Nicholas.

"Everybody just be quiet!" Cassandra screamed. She put her hands over her ears and squeezed her eyes shut. "I can't think unless I pace. And right now, I have to figure out how to get both of you out of my hair."

Nicholas spoke in a quiet voice. "Cassandra, please sit down. I want to explain what happened."

"No," she said, her sad eyes linking with his gaze. "I don't want your explanation. I want you out of here." Tears threatened, but she held them back. She thought it was painful leaving him the first time. A second time would destroy her.

"Just sit, please," he said. "If you still want me to leave after ten minutes, I promise I will, and I'll never come back. It'll kill me, but if that's what you want, I'll do it."

The pain evident on his face made her heart sink. "Fine," she said, pulling out the chair next to Melanie. "You have ten minutes." She tapped her watch face. "Clock's ticking."

Nicholas swallowed hard, took a deep breath, and leaned over the table. "First, I want to tell you how truly sorry I am about what happened in Arizona. I swear I knew nothing about the original shipment arriving on time."

Cassandra stood and pointed toward the door. "Out. Now. I'm not listening to this. You lied to me. You betrayed me. I got back home and calculated how much I lost from your order. It totaled a full month's wages. All because of your scheme."

"Actually, it wasn't because of him," Melanie said.

Cassandra turned to face her sister. "Mel, you don't know what you're talking about. I saw the boxes at Sterling. He lied to me. To us."

"I didn't lie," Nicholas said. "Your sister and Dolores sabotaged the shipment."

Cassandra looked at Nicholas with her mouth hanging open, then back at Melanie. "You? You did this?"

Melanie bit her lower lip, her eyes silently begging Nicholas for help.

He gave her a slight grin, then turned back toward Cassandra. "When Dolores came into your shop and met you, she fell in love with you. She knew you were meant for me. But she also knew I was only out of the military temporarily, that I wanted to join the Reserves after I got Sterling under control. She and Melanie hit it off, too, and Melanie told her how you wouldn't date anyone because of all the work you're doing to keep this place afloat. They concocted a plan to get us together."

Cassandra looked back and forth between Nicholas and Melanie, trying to decide if he was telling the truth.

Melanie shrugged her shoulders. "When Dolores told me how awesome Nicky was, I was sold. All you do is work. You need a little love in your life."

"The shipping office played along," Nicholas continued. "They made sure the shipment arrived when no one was at Sterling except Dolores and a key."

"But...how could you?" she said, turning to Melanie. "How could you?"

"I just want you to be happy," Melanie said, taking Cassandra's hand in hers. "I want you to have more than just me and the store. I want you to have a real family. I want us to have a real family."

Nicholas stood and held up a finger. "Give me a second. I'll be right back. Please don't go away."

Cassandra sank down into her chair, trying to assimilate what she'd heard. "I'm not going anywhere," she whispered. "Nowhere to go."

Nicholas sprinted out the door and came back moments later with a large bag in one hand and a breathtakingly beautiful crystal vase housing the world's largest bouquet of purple violets in the other. "These are for you, Cassandra. I'll forever associate violets with you...and the moment my heart became yours in Dry Creek." He set the arrangement on the table and pulled up a chair next to her.

"And this is for both you and your sister." Nicholas pulled a large photo album from the bag and set it on the table. "Cassandra, we have so much in common. We're both determined, both came from foster homes, and both crave real family. I was lucky enough to be part of one, and I want to give you part of your family back."

"I don't understand," she said, looking at the album, then up into his eyes.

"Open this, and I think you will."

She slowly drew back the cover of the leather bound book and took in a quick breath. She looked at the first page, then glanced up at Nicholas. She and Melanie thumbed through page after page, intermittently crying, then laughing as they fingered the aged photos filling the pages: their mom covered in flour; their dad tasting the cookies she held out for him.

"I should have come to see you sooner...as soon as Dolores fessed up to the sabotage. But I needed time. Time to realize what I want in my life. Time to realize I want you in it. And I wanted to bring you a gift, one that will hopefully fill the void you've felt for so many years. So I did some research—a lot of research. I looked through every regional newspaper I could locate in the records of so many towns that I lost count. I talked to every lawyer I could find and visited every archive there is to locate everything I could about your parents." He let out a deep breath. "It's all in here."

Cassandra ran her fingers across the last page. It held a picture of her standing beside her dad, Melanie on her mother's hip. "That's us. With Mom and Dad. I remember that day. It was...."

"I know," he said. "One week before the crash. I know I can't bring them back, but there's one thing I can give you. A new family—a family that loves you more than life itself. And a lifetime of love. I've decided not to go into the Reserves. I finally figured out that's not what I've been searching for. I've been searching for you."

Nicholas withdrew a blue velvet box from his pocket, lowered himself to one knee beside her, and opened the box to reveal a shimmering marquis-shaped diamond. "Cassandra, I know we've only technically been with each other about a day-and-a-half, but I can't imagine living this life without you by my side. You are my true heart's desire. Will you please give me the honor of being my wife? Being my family?"

Cassandra looked down at the image of her parents, now etched in her memory, then back at Nicholas. The love she saw there was a mirror image of the love in her parents' eyes. She knew it was true.

"Yes." She flung herself into his arms and felt at home for the first time in over two decades. "Yes, I'll marry you!"

"Now that's the way it's done," Ralph said, high-fiving Ed.

"I knew he had it in him," Ed said, slapping Ralph on the back. "Our boy's done good."

Melanie pulled her phone from her back pocket, tapped in a number and held it to her ear. Grinning like a kid on Christmas morning, she screamed. "Dolores! We did it!"

EPILOGUE

"That concoction should be illegal." Cassandra placed the last bite of the French confection onto Nicholas's tongue. Electricity danced over his skin as she gently cleared a stray remnant of chocolate glaze from the side of his lip and licked it from her finger. "It's so much better than in my fantasies."

"Paris always is," Nicholas said, trying to regain his breath. "And so are you." He shifted toward her, drawing her into a long, sensuous kiss that tasted of chocolate and vanilla. His heart ached for more than just one lifetime with this fascinating woman. Loving her, he was finally at peace.

Nicholas twirled her around the Champs-Élysées café, gently returning her feet to the ground, giving her a direct view of the stately Arc de Triomphe. Cassandra laughed. It was a sound Nicholas would never get enough of. He had worked long and hard to help her overcome her fear of flying so they could travel to

69

Europe for a chocolate-inspired honeymoon. It took six months, but they were finally in the City of Light, courtesy of a spacious 747.

***

"I, Cassandra Baker, am actually in Europe!" She squealed as she wrapped her arms around Nicholas, then placed a quick kiss on his cheek before rushing back inside to select another pastry from a fresh batch of French delights lined up on the wooden counter.

The first item on her honeymoon "to-do" list was checked off: she savored a decadent éclair au chocolat in a Parisian café. The oblong pate à choux pastry creation, filled with vanilla crème patissière and topped with a chocolate glaze, was downright sinful. The pastry chef graciously sat with Cassandra and Nicholas at their table, explaining the intricacies of French chocolate-making, from the use of pure cocoa to the rare fresh infusions of flavor, from chestnut to champagne.

She could hardly wait to explore the city and its numerous chocolate boutiques. Truffles, pralines, ganaches, and a cache of stolen kisses would fill their days before they would board a train bound for Italy and her first traditional cremino tasting. After a week learning from chocolatiers in the various regions of the romantic country, Nicholas would whisk her off to

Switzerland for chocolate bon-bon tastings and more meetings with famous confectioners.

Listening to the sound of locals chatting in their native language, she glanced around the red and brown-hued café until her eyes met with those of her husband of two days. She grinned as she thought about how much her life had changed since she'd met Nicholas.

"I can't believe I'm actually here—in France—learning from the crème de la crème of chocolatiers!" She gave Nicholas a silly grin, then walked around the café filled with chocolate treats, unable to stand still. She breathed deeply, taking in the rich, thick scent of melting chocolate being transformed into delicacies. She bit down on a smile, then couldn't hold in her happiness any longer and giggled like a schoolgirl. She couldn't wait to try out the new recipes that swirled through her head.

"We should definitely come back to Paris next year for Valentine's Day, darling," Nicholas said, sipping on a steaming beverage from a dainty porcelain cup.

Cassandra was continually amazed at how she loved this caring, tender, confident man more every day. How was that even possible? Her feet may have been back on the ground, but her heart soared to new heights with every passing moment. She looked deep into the most beautiful chocolate-brown eyes on the planet and gently kissed lips that tasted of café au lait mixed with a healthy dose of warmth and love.

"Nicholas, with you, every day is Valentine's Day."

RECIPE

HEART'S DESIRES
Original Recipe by Cadia Cox

Ingredients:

1 cup milk chocolate toffee bits (Heath)
1 cup dark chocolate chips
1 tablespoon butter, salted
1 teaspoon coconut oil (solid, if possible)
Dash of cayenne pepper
Dash of sea salt
½ teaspoon almond flavoring
Edible heart-shaped decorations
½ teaspoon pink Himalayan salt

Instructions:

Grind toffee bits in a food processor until they become a powdery consistency.

In a separate pan, melt the dark chocolate chips over low heat.

Add butter and coconut oil to melted chocolate and stir over low heat until dissolved. The mixture will thicken. Remove from heat.

Add cayenne pepper, sea salt, and almond flavoring into the batter and mix thoroughly. The batter will become just a bit thinner.

Stir in toffee powder and mix thoroughly.

Place a spoonful of mixture into heart-shaped candy molds.

Refrigerate for two hours, then remove chocolates from molds.

Add edible decorations to chocolates.

Sprinkle a few grains of pink Himalayan salt on top of each chocolate, if desired.

Keep refrigerated until ready to serve.

Makes approximately three dozen small Heart's Desires, with a bit left over for licking the bowl—my favorite part of baking! Enjoy!

DOUBLE SHOT
OF LOVE

A Coral Cove Halloween Romance

CADIA COX

Ten Story Books, LLC
Dallas, TX

For Mandy and Mr. Jake,

the two most loving dachshunds ever born.
Thanks for sharing your sweet kisses,
your unbridled joie de vivre,
and a lifetime of unconditional love.

I love and miss you both...

CHAPTER ONE

"Full time in Arizona, my ass." Melanie Baker bit her tongue at the bitterness in her own tone. She gripped the phone, winding an auburn tendril around one finger until the curl tightened like a Chinese finger trap. Nervous habits were hard to break. The call from her twin sister and business partner, Cassandra, was not going how she had hoped. Her insides twisted as tight as a pretzel. She popped a pumpkin-spiced truffle into her mouth—another nervous habit that kept her curvy stature, well, curvy.

"Please don't be upset, Mel," Cassandra said. "I know you wanted us to be in Texas full-time, but Nicholas just found out his VP of Operations is moving to Alaska to take care of his mother. You remember Cole, don't you?

"The best man at your wedding?" Melanie rubbed her temples, trying to stave off the throbbing that assaulted her skull.

"He's a really nice guy—definitely cares about his family," Cassandra said. "Anyway, his mom fell this week and broke her hip in four places, poor thing. It's going to be a really long recovery, and he doesn't think he can rightfully keep his current job if he's going to be so far up north. That means Nicholas is going to have a ton of work to find a replacement, not to mention managing his expansion plans."

Melanie smirked, boosting one of her dimples higher than the other on her rounded face. "I get that. I just don't understand why you guys can't be here at least half the time. Can't Nicky expand Sterling into Texas?" She'd expected her sister and her new brother-in-law to live in Coral Cove after they returned from their blissful Parisian honeymoon. So much for assumptions.

A sigh wafted across the phone line. "I wish he could, but with their current plan, it will have to be into California first. Besides, I thought you were okay running the business on your own. Isn't that what you said?"

Curling her toes inside her favorite Tony Lama boots, Melanie shifted to lean on the marble counter. Baking sheets boasting ingredients from caramel nougat to cinnamon and cocoa covered the display like a checkerboard tablecloth. She swiped a finger through a swath of hazelnut chocolate spread, savoring its nutty, sweet flavor. "I thought I wanted to. It's just...you know I'm no good at coming up with new recipes...and it's so lonely here without you."

"Are you kidding?" Cassandra's voice squeaked. "You're the life of every party in Coral Cove and you know it. You've got more friends there than I could ever wish to have. Hell, you and Sophie are almost as close as we are. You lonely? Get real, sis. You can do better than that."

She could, but she didn't want to. She wanted her sister there. Melanie didn't cope well with being abandoned. The acid roiling in her stomach drove her to reach for a chunk of peppermint. Hopefully it would quell the nausea. Her sister was deserting her *and* Decadent Desserts. Change can be a bitch.

"Guess I'd better get to the morning baking," Melanie said, longing to end the call and the torture.

"Mel, I hate that you're upset. I can hear it in your voice."

"I'm fine," Melanie said, nudging an auburn curl behind her ear. "Just need to get to the chocolates. You know how busy Monday mornings can be."

Right on cue, the bell above the door tinkled as Ed and Ralph shuffled into the shop.

Ed smoothed back the remaining white strands of hair on his almost bald head and collapsed into a red chair.

Ralph hooked his wooden cane on the hall tree by the door, shrugged out of his flight jacket, and made his way to the vintage sofa beside Ed, lowering himself onto the cushion.

"Look, I've got to run," Melanie said. "Ed and Ralph just got here."

"Oh! Tell them hi for me and Nicholas."

"Will do. Talk to you later. Love you."

"Thanks for understanding, Mel. Love you, too."

Melanie tucked the phone under the counter and applied her best smile for the pair of World War II veterans staring at her.

"What's up with Cassidy and her fly boy this mornin', Mel?" Ralph asked. His eyebrows lifted at the prospect of hearing the latest gossip about the blonde with a penchant for creating his favorite chocolates and her ex-Air Force pilot husband.

Melanie was still working through the major change that Cassandra had just laid on her: she was stuck in this tiny town with their "family" business. *How can it be a "family" business if there's only one of us here?* She tamped down her frustration and turned toward her two most loyal customers, treating them to a couple of her trademark dimples.

"Seems Cass and Nicky are going to be full-time Arizonans now. Looks like you two are stuck with me." She winked at the pair, trying to mask her disappointment.

Ed cleared his throat, then coughed and sputtered. "Well dang, Mellie. We were hopin' Cassidy would be back when we told you about...." He cut his eyes downward and began fidgeting with his thick fingers.

"About what?" Melanie grabbed a box of fresh sea salt caramel chocolates and rounded the counter to pull up a chair beside them. "Are you two okay?" She positioned the box on the heart-shaped coffee table and placed her smooth hand on top of Ralph's wrinkled one. "Is it your heart, Ralph?" She furrowed her brow, her head swiveling between them like she was watching the finals at Wimbledon.

Ralph patted his free hand on top of hers. "No, my dear. My heart's pumpin' along just fine. It's Ed here. He's...well...I think he should tell you."

Ed shifted on the red velvet cushion and cut his eyes toward Ralph. "I think you should tell her."

"No, it's your story. You should tell her."

"Really, it should be you."

Melanie interrupted their banter. "Would somebody *please* tell me what's going on?" She felt her own heart picking up speed.

Ed scratched his forehead, then pulled on his drooping ear. "I didn't want to tell you this, Mellie, but Ralph insisted."

"No I didn't, you crazy fool."

"Yes you did, you two-bit sergeant."

"No I didn't. Just because you outranked me in the war doesn't mean you outrank me here."

"Does too."

"Does not."

"Does too."

"Does not."

"Argh. Just stop it." Melanie said, wringing her hands to keep from losing her temper. "Would one of you *please* tell me what's going on? You're scaring me here." Her heart hammered against her chest, reverberating its way down into her belly.

Ed looked slowly toward Ralph who nodded at him. Letting out a deep breath, Ed spoke.

"Jack's back."

***

Jack Peterson hated dogs. Not that he wished them any harm; he simply couldn't stand their piercing barks and how they left fur all over everything. Then there was their yipping and drooling. But something about the stray that cowered by the country road made him pull over and take mercy on it.

Gravel crunched under the tires of his old Ford truck as he slowed it to a stop. Sliding the gear shift into park, he leaned forward to glance up at the overcast sky. "Damn rain. You'd think I was still in Seattle." He grabbed his denim jacket lying on the passenger seat and shrugged into it.

Movement in the rear-view mirror caught his eye. The drenched red-haired dachshund puppy crept close to the truck. It looked like a wet rat, hunkered over and trembling. Then it sneezed.

"Just pick him up and take him to the closest shelter," Jack advised himself, letting out a frustrated breath. He opened the door that needed a generous dose of WD-40 and unfolded himself from the worn driver's seat. His boots landed in a puddle, splashing water on his jeans. "Perfect. Absolutely perfect." He knelt down and clenched one fist in the gravel, then peered underneath his truck.

The puppy stared at him and whimpered.

"It's okay, wiener dog. Just be calm. We're gonna get you to a nice warm place if you'll trust me. Come here, boy." He extended his hand, but the movement startled the pup and it backpedaled until it hit the tire with its rear end and yelped.

"Okay, okay. Just stay right there." Jack stood up, shook the rain from his brown hair, and reached in the cab for the drive-through burger he'd just purchased. Pulling back the thin paper wrapper, he caught a whiff of grease, pickles and ketchup. "I was so looking forward to eating you," he said, tearing off a small piece of meat.

Kneeling back down, he tossed it toward the puppy who sniffed, then gobbled up the burger.

"Thaaat's it," Jack said in a calm voice, ripping off a second piece and aiming it toward a spot nearer to him.

The puppy crawled close to the ground, eyed him, then grabbed for the bait.

"You like the burger, don't you, fella? Come get some more." He tossed another piece near the tire beside his boot.

The dog lunged for it.

Jack rubbed his calf muscle that was knotting on him. "I'm gonna get a Charlie horse if you don't come out of there soon," he told the stray.

The dog perked up its ears.

"Is that your name? Charlie? Do you like that?"

The pup wagged its tail and shook, sending its ears into a flapping frenzy and lifting its back feet off the ground.

"Come'ere, boy." He held out another bite. "Here, Charlie."

Charlie crept closer, sniffed Jack's hand, then licked up the meat with one swipe of his tongue.

"Oh, that's just gross," Jack said, trying not to scare the creature by flinching. "But I'll let it go this time if you'll let me pick you up." He held out his hand, knuckles first, for the puppy to sniff, then turned it over and placed it on the ground, his palm as inviting as a doggie bed.

Charlie crept forward slowly and crawled in.

"Good boy," Jack said, stroking the wet dog's head.

Charlie reached up and lunged for Jack's lips.

"Ugh." Jack swiped his sleeve against his mouth, trying to remove all remnants of the slobber. "No kissing, Charlie. We barely know each other."

Charlie wagged his tail and nestled into the crook of Jack's arm.

"Jesus, you're even tinier up close. You can't be over six weeks old." Jack rubbed the pup behind its wet ears. "Let's get going, boy. We gotta stop by Uncle Ed's before I get you to the shelter. Can't keep the old codger waiting much longer."

Jack stepped up into the cab and lowered his arm to the bench seat, allowing Charlie to find a favorite spot to lie down.

Charlie walked around in a circle, sniffing and licking everything in the cab before nestling up against Jack's leg.

"I can't believe I'm rescuing a dog," Jack said. He slipped out of his jacket and laid it over Charlie. "Hope this keeps you warm until we can get you dried off. Maybe Uncle Ed will know what to do for you."

The back wheels spun in mud until the truck lurched forward, spewing gravel behind. Large drops of rain splattered across the windshield during the ten-minute drive into Coral Cove, reminding Jack of his last six years in Seattle.

He flicked on his blinker and pulled into his great-uncle's driveway.

Ed was rocking in a white cane rocker on the wrap-around porch surrounding the Victorian house Jack had grown up in.

Stopping just short of the porch, Jack unbuckled his seatbelt and gently cradled the denim jacket with its precious cargo still asleep underneath. He opened the door slowly so as not to awaken Charlie, but the hinge squeaked, startling the pup who started barking.

"Well, there's a sight for sore eyes," Ed said. "Whatcha got there, Jackie? Looks like that jacket of yours is gonna sprout wings and take off."

Jack huffed out a breath and said, "You like dogs, don't you, Uncle Ed? Wouldn't you like a sweet little wiener dog to keep you company?" He pulled Charlie out from under the coat and placed the wiggling body on the ground.

"Very funny." Ed scratched his belly with a fistful of chunky fingers. A smile spanned the width of his round face, exposing a couple of missing teeth.

Charlie spotted a squirrel and, suddenly energetic, chased it up a tree, then clawed at the bark, attempting to scale the hundred-year-old oak.

"Come on, you mongrel." Jack reached down to grab Charlie and tried to keep the puppy from slobbering all over his t-shirt. He tucked the dog under his arm like a running back and approached the porch. "Go see your uncle," he said, placing Charlie on the top stair and nudging him toward Ed with gentle fingers.

Ed clapped his hands on his thighs and whistled, beckoning the pup.

Raising his six-foot-two frame, Jack looked around the yard he'd played in as a kid—a rambunctious, "always looking for trouble, always looking to escape" kind of kid. His parents had moved to Coral Cove to live with his great-uncle just before Jack was born. He was the odd boy on the block, never wanting a dog. He only wanted to get away—far away—with Lanie.

And he had left, but without the second half of his heart. He'd tried to make it work without her. He'd tried to banish her intoxicating scent from his memory, along with the feel of her curves pulled close against him. It hadn't worked.

So he'd made the only choice he could: to come back home. He stood with his hands securely settled on his hips and watched the puppy try to jump up into Ed's lap.

Charlie fell on his back and rolled over, popping up only to try and fail again.

"You'll get there one of these days," Jack said, reaching down to gather up the pup. He placed the wriggling puppy into Ed's waiting hands. "You just have to wait till you get a little more height on those scrawny legs of yours."

"He's a cute one, that's for sure," Ed said, stroking Charlie's head. "Whatcha gonna do with the little fella?"

"He's getting a new home at the shelter at eight a.m. in the morning," Jack said, sinking into the rocker beside Ed's.

Ed shook his head. "Not gonna happen."

"Of course it is," Jack said.

"Shelter's full."

"Then I'll drive him to the county shelter."

"It's full."

"I'll drive him to a Houston shelter if I have to."

"They're all full."

"What happened here? Have they had a mass birthing of dogs lately?"

Ed ran his rough hand across Charlie's soft fur. "The hurricane displaced more animals than there are homes for. It was on the news last night. Don't you keep up with anything?"

Jack groaned and narrowed his eyes toward the dachshund. "You mean I've got to keep him till a space opens up?"

"You got it, Jackie. Consider yourself a dog owner."

"Not in this lifetime," Jack said, rising from the rocker to pace the length of the porch. "Thanks for letting me stay here till I can find a place I like."

"Mi casa es su casa, Jackie," Ed said, a smile rising to his lips. "Always has been. Always will be."

Jack felt the lump in his throat growing larger by the second as memories flooded his mind: Ed teaching him to fish, comforting him at his parents' funeral, supporting him when he made the hardest decision of his life.

Ed broke the silence. "Come on, Jackie. Man up and admit it. Deep down, you're a sucker for dogs."

Jack chuckled and shook his head. "Gotta get my stuff unloaded, then head over to the bar." He plucked tiny red hairs from his shirt. "Can you look after Charlie for me?"

"That's a negative. My bursitis is actin' up." Ed rubbed his knees. "I must say, it's brilliant to open an espresso bar here. It's all the town's talking about. And with your exceptional good looks, which run in the family, you know," he waggled his white brows, "you'll have all the women of Coral Cove addicted in no time."

Except for the only one I want, Jack thought. An image of his fiery-tongued, gut-clenching high school love danced through his head. He'd relished living in Seattle, but it lacked one distinct ingredient: a certain pair of emerald eyes coupled with a laugh that twisted his insides. He couldn't get Lanie out of his mind, not even after more than half a decade.

"You should get an artsy bowl to have water out front for people's dogs," Ed suggested.

"In your dreams," Jack said, turning toward his truck.

"You make sure to feed that pup and give him some water. Maybe stop by Decadent Desserts and get him a dog-friendly treat." Ed rose, shuffled toward the door, turned, and winked. "And Jack, be sure to tell the owner hello for me and thank her for the chocolates this morning. They were downright sinful. Just like her."

CHAPTER TWO

The fiend. The bastard. The heart-stomper. How dare he move back to Coral Cove? Melanie watched Jack kneel on one knee to place a tiny dachshund near a bush, tying a red leash to a balustrade on the porch next door. *He hates dogs. Why does he have that precious animal with him?* Melanie saw him bend to reach for a handful of screws with one hand. With the other, he grabbed a wooden sign with orange-painted words surrounding a pumpkin motif.

"The Jack O'Lantern. Of course." She rolled her eyes and clenched her fists hard enough to rival the turmoil tangling in her belly. "He hasn't changed a bit. Has to have *everything* be about him. What a crock of shit." Her curses were drowned out by the reverberating walls, courtesy of the bastard's drilling. *He's going to wake the dead with that thing.* She laid her hands against Decadent Dessert's stained-glass door and squinted her eyes, glaring at the wall his place shared with her chocolate shop. *How dare he?*

Jack turned and froze, then tilted his head and gave her a knee-buckling smile.

She couldn't help but admire the way his jeans hugged every curve of his ass, how his black t-shirt accentuated each rippling muscle in his tanned arms. *A shooting range has nothing on those guns.* Her fingers wiggled as they itched to turn to the dark side and run themselves through his thick mane of whiskey hair; to feel if it felt the same as it had six years ago. Her eyes ventured south and imagined what all those muscles would feel like on top of her, then perused up his body until her emerald eyes met with his dusky gray ones.

Shaking the lust from her mind, she glared at him, then gave him her best "how dare you come back and invade my territory" smirk. She whirled away from the door and plucked another pumpkin-spiced truffle from the window display.

"Can the day get any worse?" she growled, munching as she marched circles in her red cowboy boots. Her short denim skirt twirled around her knees as she stepped toward the refrigerator to withdraw a fresh batch of Heart's Desires for the afternoon crowd. The memory of her sister creating the culinary masterpiece and how it led to Cassandra finding her soul mate was about the only thing that could make Melanie smile after seeing Jack again. She was having trouble deciding whether to jump his bones or turn him in to the cops for stealing her heart and then trampling it all those years ago.

She reached for her phone and dialed Sophie, her best friend and Coral Cove's favorite hairdresser.

"The Twirl & Curl. May I help you?"

"Soph, we have to talk."

"What's up, girlfriend?" Sophie said.

Melanie groaned. She gripped the phone, begging the universe to return to normal.

"What is it, already?"

"Jack's back."

"Jack? Jack Peterson? Have you been experimenting with chocolate liqueurs this morning? I told you never to play with alcohol before five o'clock."

Melanie pinched the bridge of her rounded nose and chewed on a coconut truffle. "No, I haven't been experimenting. Or drinking. But you know the new espresso bar that's moving in next door? It's Jack's. *Jack's.* How dare he come back after what he did to me?"

"Mel, you *have* to get over him," Sophie said. "How long's it been now? Get the jerk out of your mind and move on to someone who actually *will* knock your panties off."

Melanie closed her eyes and conjured up Jack's very grown-up, very manly body doing very manly work, and now her panties were practically begging for his very manly fingers. She shook her head and pushed the lust as far as she could from her nether regions.

"It's been six years. And I know you're right," Melanie said. "But what am I going to do? My girlie parts are starting to remember how fluttery he made them back in high school."

"I hear 'ya, girl. Well...maybe you should give him a second chance. Is he as dishy as he was back then?"

"Only a zillion times dishier." Melanie sighed into the phone. "His muscles have muscles. And that tan. I just wonder how far it goes."

"Maybe you should hear him out," Sophie said. "Maybe he's here to win you back."

"When hell freezes over." Melanie remembered her last encounter with Jack and clenched her teeth.

The bells overhead tinkled. "Gotta go, girlfriend. Got customers."

Melanie plastered on her best smile, turned, and said, "Welcome to Decadent—" Her smile morphed into a grimace in record time.

"Oh. It's you."

***

Jack's grin shifted to a frown as he tried to figure out what he had done to warrant Melanie's hateful glare.

Surely she wasn't still upset about what happened in high school.

"Hey, Lanie."

Her head jerked at the nickname she hadn't heard in way too many years.

Jack leaned against the door. "I'm surprised to see you here." He broke his gaze with hers to look around her shop. "Looks like we're going to be neighbors." He grinned, shoving one hand into his jean pocket as he extended the other.

Melanie stared at his large palm, her eyes wide.

He withdrew his hand to look at it from all sides. "I wasn't paying attention and Charlie started licking them. I made sure to wash really well before coming over. Are they still dirty?"

Remembering what Sophie had said, Melanie decided to play nice. Plastering a fake smile on her face, she clasped her hands together and said, "So when did you start liking dogs?"

Jack pursed his lips as if he were trying to figure her out. *Good luck, bud,* he thought. He studied her round face and was mesmerized by the piercing green eyes highlighted by a pair of arched brows that had haunted his dreams for more than the last half decade.

"I haven't. I found Charlie abandoned on the side of the road in the rainstorm. I was going to drop him at a shelter first thing in the morning, but Uncle Ed said they're all full." He shook his head and his lips turned into a straight line. "Ed said he'd help me with him till a spot opens up, but his bursitis is pretty bad today."

"Ed has always been so good to homeless dogs," Melanie said. "I have the deepest respect for him taking in those that aren't wanted."

Jack looked like he'd been slapped. "So, how are things with your foster parents?"

Melanie's expression hardened.

Jack remembered the number of foster homes Melanie and Cassandra had been thrown between. He hurt for her. Always had.

"They're fine, I guess. They paid for one year of college for me and Cass, then had nothing more to do with us."

"How is Cassandra?"

"Oh, she's doing great. We actually started Decadent Desserts together. But she got married two months ago and lives in Phoenix full-time now. Her husband, Nicky, runs a homebuilding company out there. He's ex-Air Force. A fly boy."

Sensing her frustration percolating below the surface, he decided to change the subject. "I've missed you, Lanie."

She shifted in her boots and stared past him out the window, refusing to look him in the eye. "Um, it's good to see you, Jack. What brings you back to Coral Cove?"

She waited for an answer that didn't come. Crossing her arms over her chest, she glared at him. "I'm confused, though. You haven't called or written, or even visited in six years. *Six years*, Jack. What gives? Where've you been?"

Jack drank in her wavy auburn hair, draping over her shoulder like a 1940's movie starlet. He stepped toward her and took her hand, feeling a shiver run down his spine as her smooth skin warmed his. Jerking his head up, he recognized she had felt something too, milliseconds before she withdrew her fingers. His hand felt abandoned.

"Seattle." He drew an imaginary circle with his foot.

"Seattle?" She stomped a boot and slammed her hands on her generous hips. "You know I always wanted to go there. How dare you not contact me for six years, then march in here and think you can—"

"Lanie, I...I needed to get a few things out of my system. I had a good run of it out there. But it was time for me to come back. With what I learned, I decided to open an espresso bar here. And I kind of hoped I'd run into you, maybe see if there was anything left between us."

Her eyes shifted from bright green to a muted shade in the space of one second. *How can eyes change color that quickly?*

"No." She uttered the only word that could shred his heart. "There's nothing left between us. You took my heart and you stomped on it, then crushed it, and finished it off by abandoning me. I will *never* let you do that to me again."

Just as he was getting accustomed to the new shade of her eyes, they reverted to the brighter color that had always mesmerized him.

"I heard rumors about the espresso bar, but I didn't know it would be yours."

"With your chocolates and my espresso, maybe this can be the new 'it' area of town." At least he hoped it would be half as successful as his venture in Seattle. "Lanie, I didn't expect to see you here, next door to my bar. You always talked about leaving Coral Cove...just not with me."

Melanie cleared her throat, trying to remember why she didn't leave on the arm of the Norse God with the Grecian nose who now stood way too close for her to think clearly. Stepping back to give herself some more personal space, she searched his deep gray eyes.

"I know. I just...I couldn't. Not after you...."

She cleared her throat and changed the topic as quickly as her eyes changed shades. "Would you like to try my latest attempt? I'm working on a new recipe for Halloween." Her fingers fumbled between confections on the counter display.

"I didn't think you liked making new recipes," Jack said. "Cassandra was always the one concocting new chocolates for everyone to try in high school."

"Well, since big sis has decided not to live in Coral Cove anymore, I'm stepping up to the plate and trying to create new recipes of my own for the shop. I think I might have a hit with this one. For the holiday." Her smile lit up the room as she withdrew a few chocolates from the parchment paper lining the counter and placed them on a glass plate.

"I'd love to try it," Jack said. "What's it called?"

"Creepy Cauldrons." She lifted the plate toward him.

He carefully took a confection and sniffed it. "Interesting name." He studied the cauldron-shaped chocolate filled with celadon crème, gummy worms, eyeballs, and a pretzel mixer. Jack sucked the filling off the pretzel, then opened his mouth and tossed the cauldron in. As he chewed, his eyes started watering and his throat burned as if he'd swallowed twelve ghost peppers—whole. His reflexes made him spit it out—spewing chocolate and spit all over Melanie's chambray shirt.

"What the hell!" Melanie screamed. She lifted her arms, trying to keep them out of the mess.

"Water! Need water!" Jack sprinted toward the exposed kitchen, flinging his arms, pointing to his mouth. He rubbed his tongue across his work shirt and grabbed a glass from beside the sink, not caring if it was clean or dirty. He filled it with cool water and chugged it down. Then he repeated the process and gulped another glass of healing liquid. After another bout of coughing, he turned to her and said, "What the hell did you just feed me? Kerosene laced with cyanide?"

Melanie paraded past him as the bell announced new visitors. She laid down the dish and snatched an extra shirt. "Would you please take care of those customers? I need to go change." She glared at him, then sniffed a chocolate and touched it to her tongue as she opened the door to the back room. "Hmm. Maybe I added a bit too much tabasco."

"Ya think?" Jack shook his head and wiped the tears from his eyes. "That stuff almost killed me. You might want to rethink that particular recipe before adding it to your menu."

"I'll do that." She turned and muttered under her breath. "And you should rethink stealing hearts and stomping on them just to come back and stomp on them all over again."

"What are you talking about?" Jack said. But as much as his mouth was on fire, the fire in his belly from watching the sway of her hips rivaled it in intensity. He was drawn to her like a sugar-deprived moth to the candyland flame; always had been.

Fanning his face, he greeted the arriving customers and seized the last cauldrons from their hands before indiscreetly thrusting them down the drain.

"Hey," Melanie said, peeking around the swinging door. "What do you think you're doing?"

"Saving your sweet little ass."

"You might want to go save your sweet little dog," she said, pointing toward the window.

Charlie's leash wound around him so many times he looked like a red mummy with a shiny black nose.

Jack ran for the front door, nearly knocking the customers over like bowling pins.

"For the love of—oh, crap."

CHAPTER THREE

Three weeks.

She'd survived three weeks with Jack working next door.

Three weeks of watching sweat roll down his biceps as he hammered new shingles on the roof.

Three weeks of licking her lips each time he bent over to grab for a tool.

Three weeks of babysitting Charlie while Jack fussed and fumed about how dogs were of no use.

Three weeks of catching him rubbing Charlie's belly or scratching behind the puppy's ears when he thought she wasn't looking. The dachshund was growing on him.

Sophie stopped by Decadent Desserts during her break at the Twirl & Curl to make sure her best friend wasn't going to the dark side. The petite blonde with tight corkscrew curls bounced up the steps in a tie-dye romper and daisy flip-flops, looking like she should have been born in the 60's. She took a seat next to Melanie and her charge.

"Aw, Charlie's such an adorable puppy!" Sophie said, nuzzling the pup behind one floppy ear. "And he's getting so big. Just like his daddy over there." Sophie cocked her head toward the Jack O'Lantern.

The espresso bar currently bore no resemblance to Jack: it was gutted, seedy and hollow. But it had a lot of his charm—and probably ate half of his money.

Melanie chuckled and couldn't help but look over as Jack saluted both of them.

"So how's it going having 'grown-up' Jack versus 'high school' Jack?"

Melanie ran her hand down Charlie's soft red fur and shrugged her shoulders. "He's growing on me. Remember how he used to be so self-centered? How it was his way or the highway?" She tapped the toes of her worn tan boots on the lower step. Her denim skirt barely reached her knees, which shone in the fall sunbeams.

Sophie nodded.

"It's like he's a changed person," Melanie said. "He works so hard on that place, even asks my opinion about things. He's actually used some of my ideas. And any spare time he has, he comes over and tastes my new recipes. He mostly spits them out, but I know it's reflex, not on purpose. He even swallowed my latest creation which really did taste like a sour, molded strawberry."

"Sounds like true love," Sophie said.

"Hardly," Melanie laughed. "But it's better than I thought it would be. He's teaching me about espresso and the intricacies of brewing them. He learned all that during his time in Seattle. Remember that bar we heard about on the news? Hot Shots? He worked there."

"Seriously? Can he introduce me to the guy that started it?"

"Very funny. Seems he and the owner have a knack for espresso."

The pair munched on a selection of chocolate-covered cherries and fed Charlie some kibble.

"I think I'm falling for Jack, version two-point-oh," Melanie sighed. "I just don't know if it's the right thing. What if he tramples all over my heart like he did the last time? Or worse, abandons me again?"

"Nothing ventured, nothing gained, my friend," Sophie said. "But you know me. I'm a hopeless romantic."

Melanie and Sophie sat in silence for a few minutes, enjoying the eye candy next door until he turned and approached them.

"Hey, Sophie."

"Hi, Jack. Long time no see."

Jack looked at Melanie and said, "Way too long."

"Well that's my cue," Sophie said. "I'm out of here. Got some perms to go check on. See you two goofballs later."

"Bye, Soph," Melanie said.

"She's a good friend, isn't she?" Jack lowered his muscular body beside Melanie's voluptuous one.

"The best. Hey, why the break?"

"Thought I'd come give you a breather from Charlie."

The puppy wriggled out of Melanie's arms at the sound of his name and clambered across her lap, leaping into Jack's.

"Woah there, little fella. Take it easy."

"Admit it, Jack." A grin inched up Melanie's broad cheeks to display her dimples. "You're starting to become a dog person."

"Never," he said, scowling at the pooch, yet rubbing him behind the ears. "I wanted to ask you something. There's an espresso convention in Dallas next weekend. I was thinking about going and wondered if you'd like to go with me."

Melanie shifted on the step and bit back her first reaction, *Yes!* "I don't know. I really don't have the time." She cringed at the sound of her poor excuse.

Jack was quiet for a few moments, glancing down the street, then up toward the early afternoon sun streaming down through the maple branches next door.

"They have a ton of new chocolate shops in the Metroplex. We could stop by a few and check out the competition if you'd like."

You know you want to go. Just say yes. What's the worst that could happen? "Where's the convention?"

Jack smiled. "It's downtown. You could come with me to the tastings and demonstrations, then we could cruise to the chocolate shops. What do you say, Lanie? Take a road trip with me?"

"Just for the day?"

Jack's smile diminished. "Of course," he said. "And I'll be the perfect gentleman."

"In that case, I'd be a fool to say no," she said, chancing a glance at the man whom her head warned her against. Too bad her heart wasn't playing fair.

***

Vendors and exhibitors filled the Dallas Convention Center like a small tent city. Visitors strolled among the exhibits that drew Jack and Melanie toward their sultry scents. Jack loved watching Melanie taste each espresso: her lips barely separating when blowing a bit of the steam away from the cup. She leaned forward to inhale each aroma, then licked her delicious lips after each taste.

Jack had never wished to be a cup of espresso so much in his life.

"This is the best so far," Melanie said, pointing to the dainty cup in her hand. "I think you should look into buying from this company."

It took Jack a minute to compose himself and let his lower parts recover from the sexy way she tasted the sample. What he wouldn't give to have her sample him like that. *Down, boy.*

"Will do." He cleared his throat and tried to regain his composure. "You have a tad of cream just here." He lifted his thumb to wipe the stray froth, lingering a few seconds longer than he planned when he felt the warmth of her creamy skin.

Melanie watched as he licked the thick foam from his thumb, looking as if she wished he had removed it with his lips straight from the source.

"Thanks," she whispered.

"Lanie," he said, lowering his head toward her. He couldn't wait another moment to taste her.

She leaned back, almost imperceptibly, then ran her tongue across the gloss layering her lips.

Jack's lips met hers gently and his heart leapt as he realized she was kissing him back, not pulling away. He lifted his hands and ran them underneath her auburn curls, cradling her neck. Deepening the kiss as she opened for him, he just about fell to his knees when he heard her moan.

"Geez, you two. Get a room," a convention attendee said, trying to shuffle by them in the crowded hall.

Jack felt Melanie stiffen. He pulled back and observed her eyes, trying to read what she was thinking.

"That was...." Jack thought of what it was. *Incredible. Earth-shattering. Life-changing.*

"A mistake," Melanie said, shaking her curls. "I can't go there, Jack. Not with you. Not ever again."

Jack lowered his head and nodded, withdrawing his hands from beneath her soft curls. "I know." He raised his eyes to meet hers. "But a guy can hope."

The luster of the show dulled after Melanie's statements. He had lost her. What a fool he'd been six years ago. He should have listened to her.

Still hoping he could win her back, he decided he had to take things slow. "So, I've been thinking. Since the Jack O'Lantern's grand opening is on Halloween, what do you think about me holding a costume contest?"

Melanie stopped to thumb through some fliers at a colorful booth. "Sounds like a fun idea. Who would judge it?"

Jack opened the tri-fold brochure Melanie handed him, then refolded it and slid it into his convention bag. "I thought it would be fun for Uncle Ed and Ralph to do the judging."

She brought her hand up to cover her mouth and giggled. "Can't you see those two fighting over who the winner should be? I love those old codgers so much."

Jack chuckled. "Yeah, they're worse than Laurel and Hardy with *Who's on First*."

"So what would the prize be?"

"I was thinking free espresso for a year."

"Wow. That's quite a prize. I might have to learn to like the stuff and try to win it myself."

Jack imagined her in an array of costumes, each one a fantasy of his: the devious angel, the French maid outfit, the birthday girl modeling her birthday suit.

"Earth to Jack." Melanie waved her hand in front of his face. "Hello?"

He shook his head, wrestling his thoughts away from the fantasy fashion show. "Yeah, I'm here. Just thinking about the contest. How about visiting some of those chocolate shops now?"

Melanie smiled and nodded, her bubbling excitement making Jack's heart overflow.

"Then let's hit the road."

Jack had researched reviews for every chocolate shop in the Dallas-Fort Worth area. At *For the Love of Chocolate*, he stood back to watch Melanie running from one display counter to the next, ordering a sample of every confection they had to offer.

"You *have* to taste this apricot truffle," she said, her eyes twinkling. "I've got to figure out how to make this."

Melanie raised the chocolate to his mouth.

He opened it to accept the offering.

She stared when his tongue darted out to claim each fleck of errant chocolate powder from his lips.

Jack caught the desire in her eyes. *You still have a shot, dude. Just be patient.*

CHAPTER FOUR

Nestled against one of the small round tables he'd placed near the bar at the Jack O'Lantern, Jack watched Melanie as she reviewed his prototype menu. He yearned to reach out and tuck a stray curl behind her ear...to run his fingers along the nape of her neck...to have her welcome him with open arms.

Ever since the trip to Dallas, she had become more distant. He couldn't put his finger on it, but it felt like she had gotten too close to falling for him and decided to pull back. He believed the attraction was there, but it wasn't going to be easy to break down her barriers. First, he had to gain back her trust.

"So, what do you think?" Jack asked.

Melanie leaned back to stretch her neck and stroked Charlie's back. She rubbed her boots against the worn wooden floor, then propped them on the seat beside her. "It looks really good," she said. "I like the flavor infusions and the graphics you designed. The pumpkin is fabulous. So is the likeness of you. When did you become such a good artist?"

Jack shrugged his shoulders. "Found I had a knack for it when I was fighting through learning the ropes at Hot Shots."

"Well, you're good. Really good."

Jack wished she meant him, not his business acumen. After a month of seeing her next door every day, watching her infectious smile as she waited on her customers, and wishing he were a dog every time she stroked Charlie's fur, he realized there was a hole in his heart that only the feisty redhead across the table could fill.

He knew he had to go slowly with Melanie, but he had to start somewhere. "Hey, Lanie. Can we talk?"

She shifted in the chair, then glanced out the window, mesmerized by the red and orange leaves rustling in the breeze. "Sure. About what?"

"About us."

She whipped her head around to face him. "There is no 'us', Jack."

"But there could be," he said. "We were so good together in high school. Why can't we get part of that back?"

Melanie's cheeks flushed, just like they used to when she and Jack slid from second base into third. Then the blush dissipated as quickly as snow in sunshine. "Because you left me. You abandoned me. I can't take the chance of you leaving me again."

"Leaving without telling you was a mistake." Jack reached out to cover her hand with his, but she withdrew it before he could feel her heat.

"Ya think? Look, Jack. I'm doing my best to be friends here. We've got businesses next door to each other, and I want to play nice. Part of me wants there to be more, but it's hard to fight the memories."

"What can I do for you to give us another shot?" Jack watched as she closed her eyes, her dark lashes shading the delicate skin under them. He saw her barely shake her head before she exhaled a deep breath and slowly opened her eyes.

"Let's just work on the 'friends' part for now, okay?"

Jack nodded, willing to do anything to win her back.

He lay in his big, empty bed alone each night, remembering every move she made that day. Every word she said. Every look she sent his way. Then he fell asleep, dreaming of the feel of her lips on his, her fingers stroking his skin, sinking into her heat, then jolting awake in a cold sweat to find himself alone.

Years ago, he had thought leaving Coral Cove was the answer to all his problems. But now, he knew it was the reason for them.

***

The salty surf lapped at Melanie's toes as she and Jack waded along the Gulf coast. Pelicans soaring past cast their shadows around them. A pod of dolphins played about fifty yards offshore, and shorebirds ran back and forth, trying to grab a morsel to eat while not getting swamped by waves.

The past few weeks had seen a lot of long hours. Jack had asked for her opinion a thousand times, trying to make the best decisions for the bar. Every time he glanced her way, spoke to her, or stared at her when he thought she wasn't looking, Melanie felt closer and closer to him. She sensed herself falling and didn't know what to do about it.

Sophie kept telling her she should go for it; how many times would she get a second chance?

But she was terrified Jack would leave her again. He'd done it once. What would happen if they got into another big fight? Would he walk away then too?

Jack unhooked Charlie's leash and let him chase the birds. He squeezed Melanie's hand and kicked up the surf in front of her. "What's going on in that pretty head of yours?"

Melanie watched Charlie run after a bird, then get broadsided by a wave and pounce back out, shaking and flapping his ears. "Not much, just thinking about our businesses." She cocked her head and looked at him.

"Isn't it odd we ended up with places next to each other?"

"It's heaven for me, being so close to you," Jack said.

She squeezed his hand. "I'm starting to think the same thing."

"Seriously, Lanie, can't we try and make a go of it?" He swept his hand beneath her curls and gently rubbed his thumb across the sensitive skin behind her ear.

Melanie watched Charlie dart in and out of the waves. Being with Jack on the beach without a care in the world made it tempting. So tempting. She felt him draw her shoulder toward him as he hugged her and placed a gentle kiss on her cheek.

Shivers ran down her spine as she welcomed his breath on her skin. How could she resist what felt so right? Why would she fight something that felt like it completed her?

She turned to face him and said, "Maybe soon. You're about to wear me down."

Jack looked disturbed. "I don't mean to wear you down, Lanie. I want you to *want* to be with me."

She scanned the beach and found a spot to sit, just beyond reach of the surf.

Jack lowered himself beside her.

Melanie sat her boots on a rock and ran her toes through the sand. "Remember when we used to come out here after dark?"

"How could I forget," Jack said, tipping his head toward an outcropping of rocks down the beach. "We practically wore out those rocks, climbing behind them to make out."

Melanie blushed, then laid her head on his shoulder. "So much has happened since then."

Jack's breath warmed her temple. "I promise I've changed."

"I know you have, Jack. But I don't know if I can forget what you did to me."

"Please give me a chance, baby," he said.

She sat silent while seagulls dipped and swooped overhead, calling out to each other. When Charlie trotted out of the surf and crawled into her lap, she stroked his wet fur as he drifted to sleep.

"I'll give it some thought."

CHAPTER FIVE

Jack walked into Decadent Desserts and felt like he'd been plunged into an oven. His lungs constricted against the heat. "Lanie?"

Charlie whimpered and rubbed his nose with a raised paw. Then he sneezed.

The sound of metal objects clashing met the pair as Jack turned to take Charlie outside where it was cooler and secured his leash to a Japanese maple. Taking the steps two by two, he barreled back into the shop to find Melanie.

"Lanie? Where are you?"

Muffled curses sounded from the back room and echoed off the walls.

Lunging through the saloon doors separating the back room from the main area, Jack froze as he saw her standing in nothing but her signature boots, a thin camisole, and cutoffs straight out of a country song. She had twisted her hair into a hastily done up-do that had strands framing her head and shoulders, looking like she had just rolled out of bed from a night of unbridled passion. The temperature rose about twenty degrees as his jeans shrank a couple of sizes.

"What happened, Lanie?"

She turned to deliver him a piercing glare that would scare off most mortal men.

But Jack wasn't most men. "Lanie?" He approached her slowly and placed his hand on her shoulder.

"Damn it to hell," she swore. "I can't get the air conditioner to work. All the chocolates are going to melt, not to mention the supplies that are going to be useless if I don't get this fixed. Thanks to that and the heatwave that decided to invade Coral Cove last night, this place is hotter than hell." She grumbled some more curses then threw a screwdriver at the offending piece of machinery. Slumping toward the wall, she covered her face with her hands.

Jack stepped next to her and tucked several strands of hair behind her ear, freeing them from the sweat glistening on her neck. He reached his arm around her shoulders, hugging her close.

Melanie pulled away from him and thrust her hands on her ample hips. "I'm done," she proclaimed. Marching toward the door, she pulled a tank top off the hall tree, shrugged into it, and marched out of the shop.

"What do you mean 'done'?" Jack followed her outside, wiping sweat from his brow as he went.

"I mean done. Finished. Fini. Terminado. I quit."

Jack rubbed his jaw and tried to keep up with her train of thought. But each time he thought he had her figured out, her train departed for a foreign station.

"I'm closing up shop."

"But you can't—"

"I can, and I will." Melanie flopped down in the grass. Charlie crept toward her and laid his velvety muzzle on her exposed thigh, lifting his eyes up at her. Dogs always knew when their person was hurting.

"Lanie, you can't mean it. You've done an amazing job with Decadent Desserts. You have people from all over the nation coming by Coral Cove just for your chocolates."

"Correction," Lanie said, raising her index finger. "For Cass's chocolates." She lowered her eyes toward Charlie then stroked his head. Looking back up at Jack, she managed to display a defeated smile. "You've tasted my new recipes. You know how awful they've been."

"They're not that bad," Jack said.

Melanie tilted her head toward the sky and belted out a hearty laugh. "Good one, Mister 'spit it out all over the baker and her displays.' I've tried to make it a go, but without Cass here, I've lost more money than I've made. At this rate, I'll be out of business by Christmas, especially if I have to shell out for a new a/c unit. I need to find something else to do in life. Something that won't tank when I'm abandoned *again*."

"I can help you out if it's money you need."

Melanie shifted her eyes toward him. "Oh, please. You've got your own business to suck you dry. No offense."

Jack laughed, loving that Melanie didn't hold back any punches. "None taken." He swept his thumb along her jawline, his heart reveling in the feistiness exuded by this woman: this woman with whom he was undoubtedly still in love. How could he have abandoned her? How did he live without her wit, her spunk, her moxie all these years?

"Why don't you run home and grab a shower. I'll close up for you."

Melanie gazed at the shop, the place her sister had abandoned, just like she'd abandoned her. "Don't mind if I do." She gave Charlie one last scratch, then rose to wipe off the leaves that stuck to the backs of her legs. She tossed Jack the keys.

Jack longed to follow her home, take care of her, and wipe every remnant of hurt from her heart. But he knew their relationship was hanging on like a heavy drop of rain to a thin blade of grass. He didn't want to take the chance he might say the wrong thing and lose her forever.

Still, he had an idea. A smile crossed his face as he flipped the keys in the air. "Charlie, we've got work to do."

Melanie stepped out of the cool stream of water to grab a towel from the bathroom counter. Her phone was ringing, but she didn't feel like talking with anyone and let it go to voice mail.

"Mel? It's Cass. Call me."

Melanie glared at the phone. "Not gonna happen."

It rang again.

"Lanie? It's Jack. I know you're there."

"Again, not gonna happen." She unplugged the landline and marched into her closet.

Three more calls came in immediately to her cell phone. She listened to the messages simply so she didn't have to later: another call from Cassandra, one from Jack, and the last from Ed and Ralph.

The call from the vets doubled her over in laughter. She couldn't help but play it again.

"Hey, Mellie, this here's Ed."

"And this here's yer good friend, Ralph."

"She knows who you are, doofus."

"Well, she may not know since she ain't seein' me in person."

"She does, too. Our Mellie's a smart cookie."

"I know that, and you know that, but Jackie—"

"Now don't you go sayin' ugly things about my nephew."

"*I wouldn't dream of it, ol' man.*"

"*Just keep yer trap shut and let me do the talkin'. And stop givin' me that 'pullin' the zipper over yer mouth' nonsense.*"

"*Mmmm mm hmm mm hmm mm hmm.*"

"*Fine. I'm unzipping yer trap. See here? Unzippin' it.*"

"*That's better. Let me talk to her.*"

"*Stop grabbin' the—*"

The message ended abruptly before the phone rang again. This time she answered it.

"Mellie?" Ed said. "You'd better come down to your shop. We need 'ya."

"Need me? What's—"

But Ed had hung up before she could finish her question.

Melanie tossed on a lightweight Aztec sundress and slid her feet into a supple pair of tan boots with aqua stitching. Snatching her car keys from the hook by the door, she headed for her shop to see what had Ed and Ralph so agitated.

When she pulled to the curb, she couldn't believe the throng of people lined up to get into Decadent Desserts. She jogged across the street then worked her way up the stairs and through the door.

"I'll take a dozen." A lady in red shorts nudged by Melanie and waved her hands in the air.

A man in running shorts and a gray t-shirt cupped his hands to his mouth. "I'll take two dozen."

"Two dozen of what?" Melanie asked.

"Of those amazing frozen chocolate concoctions. I've never tasted anything like them. My wife's going to definitely forgive me for forgetting our anniversary yesterday when she tastes these."

Melanie wove her way through the throng of customers and worked her way up to the counter. "What the—"

Jack's lopsided grin made her heart do somersaults interspersed with a few cartwheels. He cocked his head toward a massive freezer unit that took up residence in a previously uninhabited corner behind her glass displays.

"Two dozen Elvis Specials, comin' right up." Ed sucked in his belly and sidestepped behind Jack to fill the order. He scooped out round chocolate disks from the freezer and slid them into an insulated snack bag Ralph held up for him.

Pulling a piece of tape from the dispenser, Jack sealed the bag and rang up the sale, then attached a coupon for a free espresso come November.

"Thanks, man. You saved me," the jogger said, grabbing the bag. "These are perfect."

"No problem. Good luck with the missus. Next?"

"Jack, what—" Melanie couldn't get a full sentence in over the orders that flew by her like darts at a bar.

"Grab that set of bags for Ralph, will 'ya?" Jack asked.

Melanie passed him a handful of orange foil sleeves that Ed began filling with scoop after scoop from the freezer.

They kept repeating the process until the shop was empty of customers.

Melanie dropped into a chair and propped her boots on the coffee table in front of her. "What was that?"

Jack smiled at her. "That, my dear, was making lemonade from a bunch of melting lemons. Well, melting chocolate, and fixing your a/c and installing a freezer with a backup generator so your chocolates won't ever melt again."

Ed untied his apron then tossed it onto the hall tree by the front door. "We're out of here, you two."

Ralph patted Ed on the shoulder. "That was the most fun I've had since we filled the nose of that navy plane with fresh shrimp for the boys in France."

Ed pulled on his earlobe. "You got that right, Ralphie."

"Don't you be callin' me 'Ralphie.' You know I hate that."

"Do not."

"Do, too."

"Do not."

"Do, too."

"Quit bumpin' yer gums, Ralphie," Ed said, nudging his sidekick out the door. Turning back toward Jack and Melanie, he said, "You're a mighty special gal, Mellie. If I was fifty, maybe sixty years younger, I'd give my Jackie a run for his money." Crinkly lines emerged beside his eyes as he sent them a wink, then left the shop whistling.

Melanie laughed, then looked at Jack. "How? Why?" She waved her hands around the room.

Jack sat down in a red velvet chair and leaned toward her. "Because, 'most beautiful woman in the known universe,' I care about you. I wanted to help you. And I don't want you to think that everyone abandons you when the going gets rough. Not anymore."

Melanie's heart warmed and felt like the Grinch's when his grew three sizes. "But what were you selling all those people?"

"That's a little invention I call the Elvis Special. I chopped up the bananas that were ripening too fast and put a dollop of peanut butter on top. I took the chocolate that was already melting and dipped the bananas into it, then froze them so that they would cool people down but wouldn't melt on them. That way, you don't lose money on product that wasn't going to stay good much longer. There should be a few more frozen bananas for tomorrow, in case the forecasted cold front misses us."

Melanie grinned and felt her dimples emerge. "Ingenious, I must say. I'm impressed." It felt good, felt right, to flirt with him after so many years. "Thanks, Jack." Her fears began to fade as she realized this time he might, just might, care enough not to abandon her. Then reality invaded her thoughts. "But it must have cost a fortune. And you've got the Jack O'Lantern to think of. I don't know how soon I can pay you back."

Jack rose from the chair and knelt in front of her, placing one hand over his heart and one on her knee. "Consider it my gift to you." His smoky eyes met hers. "I'll do anything for you, Lanie. Anything in the world."

CHAPTER SIX

"Honestly, Jack, I still don't know the difference between an espresso and a Cappuccino. I'm a hot tea girl." Melanie stroked Charlie as he warmed her lap, then looked at the different demitasse cups Jack had placed in front of her.

"Then I, Jack Peterson, am here to enlighten mi'lady in the world of specialty coffee."

Melanie laughed, her hair bouncing around her head. Sometimes she reminded him of a grown up Shirley Temple: her untamed curls, her zest for life, her boundless energy.

"Please, sir. Teach away," she said, stabilizing Charlie, then shifting on the bar stool so she could see the ingredients better.

"Okay. We're going to go about this in a different way. I'm preparing you for the most delicious, tantalizing, succulent drinks you've ever tasted." He sent her a mouth-watering grin. "Ready?"

She presented him a snappy salute. "Aye-aye, sir."

Jack laughed. "Okay, Private. Here's lesson one-oh-one. Espresso is a way to prepare coffee. It's not the coffee itself."

"Seriously?" Melanie said. "My whole life I thought it was a type of coffee."

"Nope. Just a method of preparation; a base for other drinks that are made. Most people hear espresso and think of a bitter, almost burnt-flavored drink. But those are people who haven't had a properly prepared espresso." He waggled his eyebrows. "Most often, espresso companies take quite a few roasts to provide a bold flavor. It leads to a very hearty, very intense drinking experience."

He ducked behind the espresso machine between them. After he shifted several levers and switches, the machine spewed steam followed by a loud noise.

Charlie barked, jumped up, and propped his paws on the shiny teak bar.

"Easy, boy. It's just the espresso machine," Jack said.

Charlie cocked his head and wagged his thin tail across Melanie's plaid dress.

"You're going to have to get used to it if you're planning on hanging here with the big boys."

Melanie grinned as the founding member of the *I Don't Like Any Dog on the Planet Club* reached over to scratch the dachshund's head.

"Why are the cups so tiny?" she asked, steadying Charlie with one hand, lifting up a cup and examining it with the other.

Jack lathered his hands with soap and rinsed them in the sink opposite the bar. Turning back to her, he said, "Espresso is best served from demitasse cups. You don't need a lot of espresso to have an experience you won't forget. The cups are small because the drinks are small. In America, people think more is better. In Europe, they know it's quality that matters, not quantity."

Melanie nodded and watched as Jack's hands brushed delicately over a small cup. *If he would only touch me like that.*

He gently placed the cup on a matching round saucer, then slapped both hands down on the gleaming wood bar.

Melanie jumped at the sound, bringing her back from the voice hijacking her common sense.

"Okay, so there are about a dozen different types of drinks made with espresso: single shot, double shot, ristretto, lungo, espresso macchiato, espresso con panna, cappuccino, caffe latte...."

"I recognize a few of those." *They all sound so sexy, so exotic, so strong and powerful, just like him.* Hearing the passion in his voice ignited a longing that made her shake with want.

131

"Well, there's more: caffe breve, caffe Americano, iced coffee, and a multitude of flavored espresso drinks like caffe mocha, cortado, Gibraltar, dry cappuccino, and flat white."

Melanie nestled Charlie into a ball on her lap and then fanned herself with one hand. *I'm going to need to be dunked in ice to cool down soon. It's sweltering in here. You've got to change the subject, girl. Just change the subject.* She cleared her throat and tried to refocus on the coffee. "How do you remember all of your concoctions?"

He flashed her a quick grin. "How do you remember all of your confections?"

"Touché," she said, presenting her dimples.

"Even though there are all those types of espresso, you can give an order to a hundred different baristas, and you'll get a hundred different beverages."

"Kind of like giving taxes to a hundred different accountants; you'll get a hundred different returns."

As Jack's laugh rumbled across the room, Melanie felt herself being pulled deeper and deeper into a one-way trip to "JackLand."

"The definition of espresso is pretty straightforward." Jack continued teaching. "It's one ounce of coffee made from seven grams of ground coffee beans. Then you brew those beans at nine bars of pressure at around two-hundred degrees."

"Damn, that's hot," she said. *Just like Jack.*

Jack rolled up his sleeves, exposing tanned forearms made of solid man muscle, making Melanie's girlie parts weak and wobbly.

"The Italians invented it in the late eighteen-hundreds. And they made it to be drunk quickly, thus the name, 'espresso.'"

"Ah, that makes sense." *Lord, my mouth is so dry. I'd like to take a long sweet sip of him.*

"There's one thing about it: espresso is always highly caffeinated, always strong, and always delicious."

Melanie rubbed the tip of her tongue along her upper lip. *Like the Norse God standing in front of me.* She felt her willpower collapsing, her resolve faltering. *Okay Mel, just stop it. You can't give into this...this...lust. He left you, remember?"*

Jack kept talking. "The variations of espresso typically have to do with how much steamed milk and foam accompany them."

"Okay. So when do I get to try you—" Her eyes shot up and met his cocked brow. "I meant try one?" *Fine. Don't listen to yourself.*

Jack leaned closer to her over the bar. "I'll make a single espresso for you first." He shifted back and reached under the counter. "See? We have here what's called a portafilter; it's a tightly packed container with finely ground coffee. I twist this lever and force high pressure water through it like so...." He expertly pushed knobs and buttons and pulled levers. "And the espresso is extracted in small, intense amounts."

Down girl. Who knew making espresso could be such a turn on? Pushing and pulling, pushing and pulling....

"Let me demonstrate. Here's a short shot, otherwise known as a ristretto. It's the first three-quarters of an ounce of espresso extracted. Many aficionados think this is the most perfect espresso there is." He handed her the drink. "What do you think?"

She inhaled the rich aroma, then slowly sipped the espresso. *It's not as perfect as you.* The intoxicating scent rising from the drink enveloped her in a cloud of pleasure. She licked her lips, savoring the smooth earthy flavor, every inch of her body on fire.

"A single shot is exactly one ounce of extract...like so. A lungo is also known as a 'long-shot' because it uses twice as much water. A double shot is two and a half to three ounces of extraction. But the trick is, when you make a double shot, it uses double the amount of coffee grounds. With the ristretto, single shot, and lungo, the barista uses the same single serving size of grounds."

Just give me a double shot of Jack and I'll be set.

"Next, we move on to the addition of milk product. Espresso macchiato is traditionally a shot of espresso with a layer of foamed milk on top. Macchiato means 'stained'; thus, the foam 'stains' the espresso. I know many places add a lot of caramel and chocolate to their macchiatos, but traditionally it only includes foamed milk...like so."

Melanie imagined licking foam off of Jack's gorgeous body. *Oh Lordy, it's getting hot in here.* She reached for a menu to fan herself.

"Now, if you want to get a little fancier, you can order an espresso con panna; that's a shot of espresso topped with a layer of whipped cream."

"Mmmm." *Okay, so I'll trade in the foam-fest for whipped cream delight à la Jack.*

"Or if you choose to go lighter, you can order a caffe breve, which is a shot of espresso with a light cream, such as steamed half and half."

Oh God. I've got to get my mind off of Jack and whipped cream. "What about a cap...cappuccino?"

"Cappuccino actually got its name from the color of the Capuchin monks' hooded robes. They wore simple brown robes with a little pointy hood that hung down their back, thus, the 'little hood,' or 'cappuccino.' It's a single shot of espresso with steamed milk and frothed milk, or foam. A third of each makes up a traditional cappuccino. Most baristas blend the milk and foam to make a thick, creamy mixture. It should have a glossy finish on top."

Melanie moaned, imagining the glossy finish on top of Jack's.... Her breath came in short bursts; she was about to hyperventilate.

"Are you okay, Lanie?" Jack reached up to tuck a stray curl behind her ear.

No...Yes...No...Yes...No...Oh just go for it. Just this once. "I'm fine," she said, slowly closing her eyes and leaning into his touch, wishing he would work his way down her body. She whimpered when he drew his hand away, but he placated her with a tap to the bridge of her nose.

"Now, for a sweeter, more mellow flavor, you can try a caffe latte. You mix around six ounces of steamed milk with one shot of espresso, then top it with a thin layer of foam. If you leave off the foam, voila: you have a flat white. And with a few subtle changes to this recipe, you come up with a café au lait or café con leche. Again, it should have a glossy finish."

Melanie had had all she could take. She leaned over to place Charlie in his doggie bed by her stool, then straightened back up and slapped her hands on the antique bar. "Enough with the glossy finishes, Jack. You're driving me crazy with all your talk of smooth finishes and frothy foam. Get over here and kiss me. *Now.*"

***

Jack froze, replaying her last words in his mind, then took a shortcut, hopping over the bar like a gymnast. He didn't say a word; didn't want to take a chance of breaking the spell she was under. Reaching behind her neck, he pulled her close, then leaned down and gently touched his lips to hers. He burned to take her fast and strong, but he knew if he did, she would retreat like a scared rabbit.

Be patient, man. Go slow. Savor every taste she lets you take.

Melanie wound her fingers into his short hair and wrapped her legs around him to pull him closer. So close that the air between them had to find another place to reside.

He moved next to the chair as she rubbed against the hardness that grew instantly beneath his faded jeans.

Oh, Jesus. Yes!

Jack memorized every touch, every stroke, every moan. Opening his eyes, he met her gaze, losing himself in all that was Lanie. He could live a lifetime on this memory alone.

He swept his arms around her, enjoying the feel of her generous curves as he lifted her from the stool. Striding toward the vintage brick fireplace across the room, he gently lowered her to the bearskin rug he'd ordered to give the area a more lodge-like feel.

"Mmm. This is so soft." She ran her fingers over the strands of fabric, then reached up to unbutton the top button on his denim shirt.

"Lanie, are you sure?" He gazed into her eyes, hoping his desire, and his control, shone through.

She nodded, the answer shining as clearly as the need reflected in the depths of her eyes. She wove her fingers through his thick hair and slowly closed her eyelids as he traced her smile with his talented tongue.

Jack didn't conceive he could get any harder than he already was, but that was before she reached down for the hem of her dress, lifting it slowly up above her sensuous knees, around her tapered waist, and then over her voluptuous breasts.

When the silky piece of fabric finally brushed past her mass of curls, everything else in Jack's world retreated into a hazy background.

"Jesus, Lanie." He took in every perfect inch of skin, the dip just beneath her ribs, and the dimples shining on each cheek.

"Help me with the rest?" she whispered.

Jack's hands shook as he carefully unhooked her lacy bra, pulling it out from under her. She raised her heaving breasts towards him. Her hands grasped his, lowering them to the last piece of peach silk begging to be removed. Rejoicing that her beauty spanned not only every delicious inch of her skin, but permeated every corner of her soul, Jack came undone as he slid the silky fabric over her boots.

He had no idea when he'd bought the thick, soft rug that the look of Lanie lying across it, her bare skin glowing in the moonlight streaming through the stained glass windows above, would be seared into his memory for the rest of eternity.

"Leave my Lama's on," she said, sending him a wink.

Jack's heart slammed into his chest. "You are so sexy laying there with nothing on but your boots." He made quick work of removing what was left of his clothing, grabbed a packet from his wallet, sheathed himself, then covered her body with his. He drank in another sensual kiss tasting of melted chocolate blended with cinnamon.

Lanie broke the kiss momentarily. She stretched back, and a grin swept her face. "Who knew making espresso could be such a turn on." She wrapped her legs around his waist, the leather of her cowboy boots cool against his back.

"Thank God for espresso," he said as he leaned down and rode them to paradise.

CHAPTER SEVEN

Jack's phone had been ringing non-stop the week before Halloween; just a few more days before the grand opening. He'd mostly ignored it, but he couldn't avoid this call any longer.

"Hello?"

"Jack, my main man. How's it going on the Gulf Coast?"

A genuine smile kicked the stress right out of Jack when he heard his friend's voice. "Grayson Sheffield. Things are going well. How's Seattle treating you?"

"It's not the same without you, Jack. But we're trying to make the best of it."

"Good to hear," Jack said. "To what do I owe the pleasure of your call? Everything okay at Hot Shots?"

Jack's head jerked toward the windows as the autumn wind kicked up against the glass panes, rattling them like ice cubes. An arctic blast had blown through Texas, leaving blustery days and frigid temperatures in its wake. Jack loved the chill in the breeze and took the opportunity to air out the bar.

"Buddy, I need you to head up here for a few days to finish up some paperwork on the sale."

"Can't it be done via fax?" Jack sorted a stack of purchase orders and filed them while he talked. He couldn't afford for anything to get in the way of the grand opening.

"Nope, not this time," Grayson said. "And I heard a rumor. You starting up a new venture down there?"

"You heard right, Gray," Jack said. "Hoping it'll take off like Hot Shots did. But my grand opening is on Halloween, and I don't have to tell you how soon that is." Placing the phone between his shoulder and ear, he opened a box of coffee and distributed the contents into the customized air-tight bins he had designed for the bar.

Grayson laughed in his deep baritone. "If anything can take off, it's something you have a hand in."

"Thanks for the show of support, bud. What else is on your mind?"

Another gust blew the screen door ajar, startling Jack, but he turned to watch it close gently on its own.

"Jack, I want first dibs on expanding your new enterprise. And getting you to move back to Seattle."

Jack exhaled the breath he'd been holding, afraid that's what Grayson had been after. "I'm not planning on expanding this time, Grayson. And you know how I feel about Seattle."

"Yeah, yeah, you missed that woman."

"Not just any woman, Grayson." Jack's eyes detoured to the bearskin rug, remembering the vision of Melanie draped across it. "The love of my life."

Grayson cleared his throat. "So how's it going with said 'love of your life?'"

"So far, so good. She's warming up to me. I'm taking things slow, trying to regain her trust. I wasn't exactly a knight in shining armor when I left."

"Don't your millions mean anything to her?"

The wind blew the screen door open again, but Jack didn't turn around. It must have blown the stack of folders off the chair next to the door as well, he figured, because he heard them scratch against the Birchwood floor.

"She doesn't know about it yet."

"Why the hell not? Isn't that why you came to Seattle? To try and make something of yourself?"

"Because I'm not going to tell her."

"Again, I ask, why the hell not?"

"I never told her the whole story, and I'm not going to start now. It's something I'm keeping to myself." Jack knew he'd have to come clean to Melanie one day, but it was still touch and go in their relationship, and there were parts of the past six years he simply didn't want to discuss with her yet.

"Whatever you think, man," Grayson said. "Just make sure you don't go keeping too much from her. I know if I kept anything from Sharon, she'd cut off my 'privileges.'"

Jack threw back his head and laughed. "Lanie would cut off more than that if she knew. I'll figure out a way to tell her...someday. Look, I think I can get away if I'm only there a day. My uncle Ed and his friend can look after things at the bar. They've taken quite a liking to it. I think he and Ralph would make great managers."

"Humor me, Jack," Grayson said. "Tell me what I want to hear."

"Fine. Here goes. I'm moving back to Seattle, starting my new franchise there, and getting married to my fiancée, Sharon."

"Oh very funny, Jack. You're just a barrel of monkeys."

"Just telling you like it is." Jack smiled, enjoying the banter with his friend.

Grayson chuckled on the other end.

"Look, I'll see if I can grab a flight tonight, but I have to be back tomorrow."

"You do that, Jack. And don't be a stranger. Sharon says you have to stay with us while you're in town. She sends her love."

"Tell Sharon she'll get her kiss and a surprise when I get there. Talk with you soon."

The wind slammed the screen door behind him. Jack hung up the phone and turned, only to see Melanie running down the stairs.

Jack sprinted out the door. "Lanie! Wait!"

The outburst startled Charlie who started barking and howling.

Melanie slammed the door of her vintage Mustang, then revved the engine and spun the wheels, flinging gravel toward him as she sped away.

Charlie ran in circles around Jack's feet, tangling them both in his extend-a-leash.

"Charlie, stop!" Jack screamed.

Charlie stopped mid-leap, dropped to the ground and cowered behind Jack who bent down to untangle the mess.

"I'm sorry for yelling, fella." Jack raised his head and stared down the road. "But I think I just messed up big time."

***

Melanie swerved to miss an eighteen-wheeler, then careened into the Twirl & Curl's gravel parking lot.

Sophie ran outside to see what had her best friend driving like an Indy 500 racer.

"What the hell, Mel? Do you have a death wish?" Sophie tried to wave away the wall of dust Melanie's Mustang kicked up around the salon.

Melanie extracted herself from the car and slammed the door. "He lied to me, Soph. I fell for it again. Do I have 'fall for the closest jackass' tattooed on my damn forehead?"

"Come with me, girlfriend. Let's take this inside to my office." Sophie put her arm around Melanie's shoulders and led her through the back door of the salon.

Melanie collapsed onto Sophie's vintage hot pink vinyl sofa and flung her arms over her eyes. The chemical aroma of perms and bleach wafted through the room.

"I can't believe I fell for the same shit all over again!" Melanie screamed. Clutching her chest, she sobbed between breaths, then felt hyperventilation toying with her lungs.

Sophie rolled across the linoleum floor in her roller chair and took her friend's hand. "Now tell me everything, sugar. Every detail. What happened? I thought things were going great for you two."

"So did I!" Melanie wailed, wiping the trail of fresh tears from her cheeks with her fingertips. "So did I." She blubbered some more, sniffled, then let out a wail that could be heard three counties away.

Sophie rolled to the credenza to pluck a box of tissues from the corner. She pulled three out, gave them to Melanie and nodded. "Continue."

"I ran over to the Jack O'Lantern to return Charlie after his walk and I heard Jack on the phone."

"And?" Sophie asked.

Melanie blew into a tissue, shaking her head as she wiped her nose. "He was on the phone with someone in Seattle. He's going back...to his fiancée!" The tears flowed in earnest as she flung herself across the sofa.

"Surely you heard wrong, honey." Sophie rubbed Melanie's arm, trying to calm her down. "Jack's in love with you. Everyone in Coral Cove knows it." She replaced her wrinkle of concern with the hint of a smile. Always the calming force.

"No, he's not."

"Yes, he is."

"No, he's in love with someone named Sharon. And he's taking a job in Seattle. He's giving the Jack O'Lantern to Ed and Ralph to run."

"Oh, good gracious. Now I know you had to have missed something. Lordy, there is no way on God's green earth Ed and Ralph could run anything."

"But I heard him say it. I was in the room." Melanie sniffled and blew her nose. Hard.

"There has to be an explanation," Sophie said, tapping her chin with one long sparkly fingernail, crossing her slim legs, and swinging one of them up and down.

"There is," Melanie said, wiping her nose. "He doesn't love me, and I've done the one thing I swore I'd never do again—fall for that jackass. I swear, Soph, everyone I love leaves me. Our parents, then Jack, then Cass, and now Jack again. Why do they all leave me?"

CHAPTER EIGHT

Driving had always been cathartic in the past, so why wasn't it helping? Miles of blacktop stretched behind Melanie like a thin winding ribbon and loomed in front of her as she tried to figure out how she had gone and gotten her heart broken by Jack...*again.*

She stared at the stale cup of coffee in the cup holder and decided against drinking it. Although it wasn't in the same league as the specialty coffee Jack had taught her to love, it still reminded her of him. She rolled down the window and tossed the liquid out, then crunched the thick paper cup in her hands and pitched it into the passenger-side floorboard.

"Bastaaard!" She clenched the steering wheel and screamed the word until her vocal chords began to hurt. How could she have fallen for Jack's pretty words and seductive touches again? Didn't she learn her lesson the first time?

Tears filled her eyes so fully that she had to exit the interstate and pull into a truck stop to calm down. All around the station, brown boulders soared toward the sky, looming like large rock statues huddling close to protect her. She banged her hands against the steering wheel and accidently blew the horn when her head fell forward. *Honk!*

Heaving from her sobs, she let the tears flow until a knock on the window made her whip up her head.

She looked out the driver's side and saw a mammoth of a trucker shuffling his feet outside her door. Grabbing the hand crank, she lowered the window a few inches.

"Are you okay, ma'am?" The man bent sideways so he could talk to her eye to eye. "I was headin' back to my truck and saw you lettin' loose on that gorgeous car of yours. Figured somethin' bad must be wrong for you to bang on her like that."

Melanie wiped her cheeks and felt them redden with embarrassment. The Mustang was a classic, and it hadn't done one thing to hurt her. That had been Jack's department.

"You're right, sir. I apologize. Just having guy troubles."

"Well, any guy that's got a lady such as yourself this upset isn't worth his salt. Life's too short to get as angry as a grizzly over such things, much less take it out on an innocent 'Stang. Either talk it out with him, or get on with your life."

Melanie let the trucker's words sink in, then she looked up at him and nodded. "You know, sir, you're right. Thanks so much for checking on me. And thanks for the advice."

"You take care now, and make sure to finish those tears before drivin' on. Wouldn't want anything to happen to that 'Stang. She's a beaut'."

"I'll make sure. Thanks again." Melanie rolled up the window.

"He's right," she told her car. "Time to get on with my life."

The Mustang ate up the westward miles, and before she knew it, Melanie saw the sunrise in her rearview mirror.

"God, I'm exhausted," she said, pulling into the driveway. The gearshift was cool in her hand as she shifted it into park and laid her head on the hard steering wheel.

During the drive, she had decided she had one of two choices: Either she could continue to base her happiness on others and try to cling to them to keep them from abandoning her; or she could make decisions based on what she wanted, and realize that people leaving would not define her life. At least that's what the latest issue of *Cosmo* she'd picked up at a convenience store along I-20 had preached and what her conversation with the trucker helped her realize.

"You *have* to tell me where she went."

"No, Jack. I don't." Sophie pulled a foil from her tray and placed it next to Mrs. Beecham's scalp. Dipping a brush into a bowl of thick purple cream, she covered it with the goo, then applied it to her client's inch-long hair. Purple was the new silver.

"Why not?" Jack begged. "Don't you want us to get back together?"

"What I want is for you *not* to break my best friend's heart *ever again*." Sophie sat the brush down, then poked her finger against Jack's chest as three elderly women under hairdryers and heat lamps watched the confrontation, twisting their heads back and forth like they were scrutinizing a tennis match.

"You know what your problem is, Jack?" Sophie wiped her hands on her smock, then turned to look directly at him. "It's always all about you. What you want others to do for you. Not what you can do for others. Mel's right. You *are* a self-centered jackass."

Mrs. Jackson raised her head from the rinse bowl. "You tell him, Sophie."

Jack looked sucker-punched. He lowered himself into the lavender salon chair next to Mrs. Beecham. "Did she really say that? Is that really how she feels?"

"I might be paraphrasing a bit, but yeah. That's it in a nutshell." Sophie placed another foil in Mrs. Beecham's hair.

"You know I love her more than anything in the world," Jack said.

Sophie turned to face him. "And you left her; skipped town when she needed you the most. That girl has been on the receiving end of more desertions in her twenty-four years than most people are in their entire lives: First her parents, then God knows how many foster homes, then you shredded her heart when you left without her. Now Cass is off in Arizona, and you have some floozy waiting for you up in rain central. Why are you planning on leaving her again? Running off to Seattle? *Engaged* to another woman?"

Oohs and aahs sounded behind them.

"I am not running off to Seattle, and I am not engaged to another woman."

"Shame on you, Jackie," said Mrs. Eldridge from under the heat lamps, shaking a wrinkly finger at him.

He turned to face his first grade teacher. "Mrs. Eldridge, I promise you, I'm not. I love Lanie."

"Then why are you chasing another skirt in another city, young man?" Mrs. Fletcher yelled from under the noisy hairdryer. For being hard of hearing, she sure followed the conversation well.

Jack looked defeated.

Sophie grabbed his shoulders and turned him to face her.

"I'm going to give you some advice," Sophie said. "And you'd best be for listening to it. If you don't want to lose the best thing you've ever known or will ever know, you'd better be straight up with Mel about every detail. She only cares about the truth, not about your millions. Not even about...Sharon."

Gasps rose behind him from their audience, then descended to whispers.

Jack went rigid. "You know about that? About her?"

"Get real. I did an internet search on every aspect of your life I could. You did a great job hiding it, but I did an even better job rooting it out." She straightened her shoulders and gave him a curt nod. "I may look like just a flaky hairdresser to you, but I'm a damn good amateur hacker."

"Does Lanie know?" he asked.

"No," Sophie said. "That's your story to tell. And you'd better tell her everything. And I mean *everything*."

"Look, Sophie," Jack said, glancing at his watch. "I have to catch a flight to Seattle. I've delayed this trip as long as I could, trying to hunt Lanie down. Will you please ask her to call me? I really need to talk to her."

"Seriously Jack? You're going to Seattle before you find her?" Sophie shook her head. "You really are a piece of work. Sometimes I just don't know what she sees in you. You'd better go after her, lover-boy. You know where to find her, Jack." She poked him on the forehead. "You just have to use that thick head of yours."

CHAPTER NINE

Melanie plucked another tissue from the box and blew.

"You're going to blow your nose off if you don't stop crying," Cassandra said. "I still can't believe you drove all the way out here by yourself. Why didn't you call? Nicholas would have sent the plane." Always the overprotective sister, Cassandra tucked a crocheted blanket around Melanie's legs and steeped her a cup of herbal tea.

"Obviously I wasn't thinking," Melanie said, shaking her head, then slapping her hands against her forehead. "All I knew was I had to get out of Coral Cove. Away from...*Jack*." The tears sprang loose again, and Cassandra opened a new box of tissues, jerking the first one out for her little sister.

"Mel, we'll figure this out," Cassandra said, rubbing Melanie's shaking shoulder. "Now start from the beginning."

Melanie repeated everything she could remember, from when she first saw Jack next door with Charlie, to having his bar next door, to how she was now incorporating espresso into some of her new recipes, all because it made her feel closer to him. Then she moved to the incriminating phone call she overheard about Sharon and Seattle. She left out the lovemaking on the bearskin rug by the fireplace. The thought of showing the depth of her feelings for Jack in such a passionate, intimate way now made her feel nothing short of embarrassed. And hurt.

"Who is this Sharon?" Cassandra asked, leaning back into a sea of pillows on the L-shaped sofa tucked into her family room. She kicked off her Converse sneakers and curled her legs underneath her.

"His—fiancée!" Melanie's waterworks broke past all the barriers again. Fighting the tears was futile.

Nicholas brought in another six-pack of tissues and laid a plate of pumpkin sugar cookies and a box of amaretto crème chocolates in front of them on the glass coffee table. He turned to give Melanie a tight hug, sent his wife a consoling look, then left the sisters alone.

"Okay, Mel, none of this sounds plausible." Cassandra snatched a cookie and sank her teeth into it, then licked orange icing from the side of her lip. Chewing the cookie, she stood up, grabbed her mug of tea, and paced the room in her Diamondbacks t-shirt, cutoffs, and bare feet. Arizona attire for sure. She paused beside the bookcase filled with cookbooks, took a sip of chamomile tea, and pursed her lips. "Why would he be courting you and starting a business in Coral Cove if he has a fiancée stashed away in Seattle?"

"I know. I know. It sounds crazy." Melanie slapped her hands on her thighs, rubbing them to make the sudden sting disappear. "But that's what I heard. Straight from the jackass's mouth." Melanie's voice cracked, sounding like a pubescent teenager.

Cassandra lowered herself onto the sofa beside her sister, wrapped her in her arms, and gave her a quick kiss on her temple. "I think you need to talk to him, honey."

Melanie leaned into Cassandra's hug, laying her head on her sister's shoulder, the last of her energy evaporating like the morning dew. Her curls sagged as she shook her head. "No. I don't want to talk to him. Ever again."

***

For the life of him, Jack couldn't figure out why he'd stayed in Seattle for so many years. Between the constant drizzle, the relentless fog, and the gray skies, he felt more depressed than ever. Especially pining for the one woman who owned his heart, but who wouldn't answer his calls.

"Jack, talk to me." Sharon ran her manicured nail over his sleeve.

"I've lost her. I've lost Lanie for good." He downed a shot of Kentucky's finest whiskey, then asked the barkeep for a double.

"Ah, the elusive Lanie." She grinned and tilted her corkscrew curls to the side. "I have a question for you. If I hadn't found your journal and confronted you about it during our rehearsal dinner, would you have gone through with it? With marrying me?"

Jack placed a hand on top of her cool one and cringed. "I was planning on it."

"But why? Why would you want to marry me when you were still in love with someone else?"

"It's complicated."

"Then un-complicate it for me."

"You're going to think I'm an ass."

"I already know you're an ass." Sharon cocked her head toward him, then leaned back and took a long sip of her martini. "So just tell me. I think I deserve to know."

Jack took a deep breath and pulled out his phone. "Lanie would like you, you know." After a few taps, he turned it to show her a photo.

Sharon gasped, flinging both hands over her perfectly applied lipstick. "Oh my word, Jack!" Her green eyes darted back and forth between the photo and Jack's forlorn face.

"Yeah, I know," he said, laying the phone on the table. "It's like you two are twins."

"Is that why you dated me? Asked me to marry you? Spend the rest of my life with you?" Sharon started breathing harder and rubbed her hands down her pencil-thin skirt.

"I told you you'd think I'm an ass."

"Oh, honey, I'm just glad I found that journal in time. Gracious—I didn't know I was a placeholder for someone. Anyway, it's water under the bridge for me at this point." She flicked her wrist nonchalantly. "I'm with Grayson now, the love of my life, and if I hadn't run out of Seattle Estates in the middle of our rehearsal dinner, I never would have gotten into the Lamborghini with your best man and begged him to drive me as far away from that place as possible. Grayson practically carried me into a five-star restaurant and listened to me blabber on about you and how you were in love with someone else but knew you couldn't have her so you thought you'd find a substitute in me. Now I know why I was a substitute: I'm a dead ringer for her."

"You're right. After you ran out on me, I realized I had to find a way to be with Lanie. And that meant leaving Seattle; selling the business."

"So why did Lanie run out on you?"

Jack took another swig of his whiskey, feeling the burn as it made its way down his throat. "She overheard

159

my phone call with Grayson yesterday. He had asked if I'd told her everything, and I told him I hadn't. I also told him I'd make it a point to get to Seattle this week and to tell Sharon I'd have a kiss waiting for her when I got there, among other things. When the call ended, I realized Lanie had overheard the whole thing, one-sided of course. And when I replayed the conversation in my head from the side she heard, it sounded pretty damn incriminating."

"Ah. And she ran."

"That she did."

"Just like me."

"You got it. Only thing is, now I can't find her. Her best friend won't tell me where she is; just that I should know."

"She's right." Sharon patted his thigh. "If you're going to be with her, be part of her family, you *should* know."

Grayson approached the table, slapped Jack on the back, then lowered himself into the booth Sharon had chosen.

She reached for her fiancé's hand. "Grayson, let's leave Jack to figure this thing out on his own."

Grayson threw back his scotch and laughed. Rising with Sharon, he squeezed Jack's shoulders. "You can do this, my friend. Believe me, when it's the right woman, she's worth fighting for."

The A-list couple exited the restaurant, leaving Jack to wallow in his whiskey.

I've tried to find her. I've done everything I can think of. He tossed back another shot and realized he'd lost the best thing that had ever happened to him. Twice.

CHAPTER TEN

Halloween arrived, and Melanie stared at Decadent Dessert's door from the sidewalk. Between spending a couple of days with her sister and driving back to Texas, she'd been able to avoid coming here, not wanting Jack to find her. But according to Ed, Jack hadn't returned to Texas until late last night.

Now it was time to get on with her life. On her terms, and her terms alone. And that meant opening Decadent Desserts up for business again.

She glanced next door to find practically the entire population of Coral Cove waiting outside the Jack O'Lantern's doors, rubbing their hands together in the cold, eager to enjoy espresso brewed by the legendary Seattle barista, Jack Peterson, himself. Seemed everyone, including Melanie, now knew of his good fortune due to a story that appeared in yesterday's paper reporting the final sale of Hot Shots and the hometown genius behind the successful bar.

She couldn't help but smile when she saw Ed and Ralph manning the costume contest table set up in the grass. They both looked dapper in their military uniforms. Ed squeezed into his green and khaki service uniform, barely getting the buttons to meet their buttonholes even after he had apparently let out the jacket to make room for his rounded belly. Ralph's uniform, on the other hand, had extra space from his loss of weight over the years. They both sported Marine green soft Garrison caps, perched to the side.

Charlie had set up camp between them, propping his paws on the wooden picnic table. An orange and black striped witch's hat with yellow confetti sprinkled across it sat on his head, and a long black cape draped over his back all the way down to the tip of his tail.

"Hello Mellie," Ed said, watching Melanie approach the table. "Whatcha dressed up as for Halloween? You're lookin' pretty, uhm...normal."

"Just not in the Halloween mood, I guess." She rubbed a circle in the dirt with the toe of her gray cowboy boot and smoothed her denim dress.

"Have you two not patched things up yet?" Ed asked. Creases formed at the corners of his eyes.

Melanie shook her head.

"You come sit down with us, Mellie," Ralph said, patting the bench beside him. "Why don't you help us judge this here contest? Charlie would like that, wouldn't 'ya, fella?"

Charlie perked up his ears, licked Ralph's arm, and wagged his thin tail under the black cape that swooshed back and forth with the movement.

"Thanks, Ralph," Melanie said, reaching over to give Charlie a scratch behind the one ear visible underneath the hat. "But I think I'll go make sure I'm ready with the chocolates in case anyone has any room left over after all that espresso they're going to be downing." She gazed at the crowd. "Looks like the whole town turned out for the opening. Maybe a few Houstonions as well."

"Seems that way, Mellie."

Ed gave pieces of paper with numbers written on them to a black cat, a whirling dervish, and a fairy princess to pin to their costumes. "Now remember, me and Ralph here are gonna announce the winner at oh-eight-hundred hours."

The princess, dressed in glittery gold from her crown to her stilettos, gave them a big smile, obviously hoping it would increase her chances at being fully caffeinated for the next year.

Melanie patted the vets on the back. "You fellas have a good time. I'm going to go open the shop. Stop by if you get hungry."

Ed sent her a wink. "Don't you fret, Mellie. I know everything will work out. Right, Charlie?"

The dachshund barked three quick barks, then whimpered as Melanie walked away.

***

Jack watched Melanie from the street.

She walked up to the door of Decadent Desserts as Charlie barreled into her feet.

"Well hi there, little guy," Melanie said, kneeling on the stair as Charlie launched into her arms, knocking his Halloween hat askew. Warm kisses covered her cheeks, and she hugged him close. "I didn't know you were going to run after me, but you're just what I need. Thanks for caring."

"I'll always care, Lanie. Until my last breath."

Melanie froze, then looked up into the smoky eyes staring down at her. "What are you doing here, Jack? Don't you have a grand opening this morning?" She nodded toward the crowd assembled next door. Exhaustion must have overtaken her, leaving her face devoid of emotion.

"It's not for another thirty minutes," Jack said. "Besides, I have more important things to handle at the moment." He shuffled his feet and tucked his hands into his jean pockets. "May I join you?"

She shrugged her shoulders. "It's a free country."

Jack sat on the cool concrete beside her, then reached out to pet Charlie.

Melanie stared beyond the street at Halloween decorations spread across the lawns. "Why are you here, Jack?"

He could see the dried trail of morning tears that must have made it through her makeup. He reached to wipe a stray remnant from her lashes, then tipped up her chin so she could see him.

Melanie cocked her head. "Why did you decide to go to Seattle six years ago? And why didn't you come back sooner, or at least try to contact me?"

Jack weighed his options. How much should he tell her? Would she run away from him or think less of him? He chose the safest answer; the honest answer.

"Lanie, you know how things were. All I wanted to do was get out of this excuse for a dot on the map. I wanted something bigger in life. I didn't know what exactly. Christ, we were only eighteen." He swallowed hard and fought the urge to take her into his arms and love all the hurt away. "But I knew whatever it was, it wasn't here. The only thing I did know for sure was I wanted to run away with you. But after the fight we had, I realized maybe I needed to get away and grow up before I came back for you."

Melanie sniffled.

Jack reached into his back pocket for a handkerchief to give her.

"You were right, you know," he said. "I *was* being immature and selfish and not thinking about our future; just mine. I was so angry that you didn't want to leave with me. But you needed to be here with Cass; she was all you had. After our fight, I went home, packed a couple of bags, hopped in my truck, and started driving as far away from Coral Cove—and from you—as I could. When I hit Minnesota, I hung a left and drove till I reached Seattle and the road didn't go any farther. It was late, but I tried to go to a bar and dull the pain. They threw me out when I showed them my ID without thinking it showed I was only eighteen. The barkeep said, 'You don't belong in here, kid. Try that coffee shop across the street.'

So I did. After drowning my sorrows in a cup of the best coffee I'd ever had, the barista taught me the ins and outs of a good cup of coffee and even more importantly, what made an exceptional espresso. I realized that I enjoyed the creative process, so I hung around that shop every day for the next week till I ran out of money. Then he gave me a job.

I learned so much in that first year that I decided to try and make a go of it on my own. I started a small espresso kiosk and called it Hot Shots. A kiosk was all I could afford, but the place caught on, and after four long years of endless hard work, I was deemed an 'overnight success' by the Seattle papers. Next thing I knew, I was getting offers for more money than I dreamed existed. Part of me was still empty, though. The part that had been empty since I'd left Coral Cove. Since I'd left you."

He shifted on the stair and took her hand in his. "I missed your feisty nature, and your sharp tongue and wit. I missed walking in the surf with you by my side. I missed running through the waves with you as you kicked up salt water and started sand fights. I missed making out with you in the back of my Ford. But most of all, I missed the second part of my heart."

"But what about your...fiancée?" Melanie bit out the word, then shivered. "How do you explain her?"

"One day I was working at Hot Shots, and all of a sudden, everything in my world felt right again." He took a chance and enveloped her hand between his. "It was the day you walked in."

Melanie scrunched her brows. "But I've never been to Seattle."

"That's just it. I thought it was you, but it wasn't. It was Sharon. She looks just like you. The spitting image." His laugh sounded sad.

"You're kidding, right?"

"Nope. She is exactly like you." He shifted his legs, then crossed his ankles. "Well, not *exactly* like you."

Melanie cocked her head to the side. "And?"

"And I asked her out. We dated for over two years, then I asked her to marry me. We were actually at our rehearsal dinner when she ran out on me. She'd found my journal the night before and read about you. Even though she looks the same on the outside, you two couldn't be more different. Don't get me wrong, she's a wonderful woman...a wonderful woman who is now engaged to my best friend."

"But what about the phone call I overheard?" She scooted closer to the door, leaned back on the jamb, and pressed her forearms against her belly.

Jack took a chance and ran his finger along her wrist. "Baby, that was totally and completely a huge misunderstanding. You see, Grayson—that's my best friend—was baiting me, and I was playing along with him. After I turned and saw you bolt out the door, I replayed the conversation in my head from your viewpoint. And honestly? I would have run too."

Melanie sniffled a couple of times.

"I ran after you, but you can really leave us mortal drivers in the dust. Anyway, after I couldn't get you to answer your phone and I couldn't find you, I tracked down Sophie, but she wouldn't tell me where you were. Said I should know. But by that time, I had no choice—I had to get to Seattle to finish outstanding paperwork for the sale of Hot Shots that I'd been putting off." He looked to Melanie for understanding, but he couldn't read the thoughts clouding her eyes. "While I was there, Sharon said something that made me realize where you had run to. So I took the next flight and ended up on your sister's doorstep."

"You went to Cass's?"

"That's right. I don't know why I didn't figure it out sooner. By the way, Nicholas is a great guy. He really raked me over the coals."

Melanie cracked a small smile.

"He loves you very much, but not as much as I do. Lanie, I know I made a mess of things years ago, and another whopper this week, but nothing and no one in the world means as much to me as you do."

Jack hoped she saw the seriousness in his gray eyes. He glanced at his watch, then lifted his head to meet her gaze. "Please say you'll come to the grand opening."

CHAPTER ELEVEN

"Happy Halloween espresso lovers!" Jack said, raising his arms high in the air, a Dracula cape swirling behind him in the morning breeze.

Vampires, witches, and storybook characters congregated by the steps leading into the hottest spot in Coral Cove.

Jack spotted Melanie at the table with Ed and Ralph. She held Charlie close, rubbing the fur behind his ear with her nose.

"I know you all are excited to try some espresso, but first, we have a couple of pieces of business to take care of." Jack waved to the vets, motioning for them to join him. "Uncle Ed? Ralph? Would you two please come up here? Everyone, please give our judges a big Texas round of applause."

The crowd cheered and clapped, whooped and hollered as Ed and Ralph climbed the stairs.

Jack leaned over to whisper something in Ed's ear, then addressed the rowdy crowd.

"I'd like to introduce you to two of my role models. My idols, actually. My great-uncle Ed Peterson, and his Marine buddy, Ralph Johnson. These two men fought bravely at more battles during the war than I can count."

Oo-rah's and cheers filled the morning air.

Ed cleared his throat, then tipped his cap to the crowd. "Mornin' everyone," he said.

"Morning Ed!" the crowd replied.

"Ralph, here, and I have tried to be objective and pick the best costume there is for this honor."

"Tell us the winner!" Frankenstein yelled from the sidewalk.

"Hold yer horses, young man," Ralph said. "He's gettin' to it."

"As I was tryin' to say," Ed continued, "there are so many fancy costumes here today, we decided we can't pick one out as the best. You Coral Covers did a bang-up job. So we decided since we can't choose, we're gonna draw a number out of this here basket."

Smiles stretched across the faces of pumpkins, doctors, superheroes, and every type of animal imaginable.

"And the winner is...."

Ralph shook the basket, stirred the pieces of paper with his hand, then held the basket up to Ed who withdrew a single slip.

"Betty Eldridge." Ed's cheeks turned cherry red as Little Bo Peep approached the stage, snagged him around the waist with her shepherd's hook, and planted a kiss squarely on his lips.

"I'd say that's worth a year of espresso," Jack said, laughing with the crowd.

***

Melanie had to giggle at the sight of her first-grade teacher planting a whopper of a kiss on Ed. He would never hear the end of it.

"Is everyone ready for the unveiling?" Jack asked.

More cheers and applause rose from the crowd.

"I know everyone was expecting the Jack O'Lantern to open today, but that's not going to happen."

The cheering stopped, supplanted by murmurs among the costumed contestants.

Melanie's puzzled look met the pair of mischievous eyes staring straight at her. "What's going on?" she mouthed.

"Thanks to the evening news, you all know that Hot Shots in Seattle was my business; my baby. But what you don't know is why I sold it and came back to Coral Cove." He placed one hand over his heart and smiled at Melanie. "I came back because I wanted another chance with the love of my life: the love that I stupidly left behind six years ago."

Melanie rubbed under her eyes as tears of happiness sprang to life.

"This better be good, young man," Mrs. Eldridge squawked, curtly nodding her head.

Jack kept his eyes on Melanie as he continued his speech. "I screwed up six years ago. No doubt about it. I was self-centered and self-absorbed. I had no clue what life was really about. But living without Lanie, Melanie to all of you, was worse than any punishment I could have imagined. However, being back here, working on opening this bar next door to Melanie's brainchild, Decadent Desserts, and having the honor of winning back the love of my life, I realized that I couldn't name the bar after me. I've turned over that self-centered leaf and renamed her." He motioned for Melanie to join him.

A blush claimed her cheeks as she climbed the stairs and walked into the embrace he offered.

"Lanie was gracious enough to give me a second shot at love. So now, I welcome you to the espresso bar named in her honor, *The Double Shot*."

Jack pulled the string attached to the canvas draping over the sign above them and unveiled the new name and logo: two hearts swirling in foam atop a cup of cappuccino.

The crowd cheered, whistling and clapping as Frankenstein bounded up the stairs and lifted Melanie over his head. With the assistance of a mummy, a ghost, and a zombie, they paraded her around the yard, then brought her back up the stairs and placed her feet on the stoop next to Jack. Then the chants began: "Kiss her! Kiss her! Kiss her!"

Melanie felt a warmth inside she hadn't felt since Jack wrapped his heart around hers in high school.

"What do you think, Lanie? Should we give them what they're asking for?"

Melanie smiled and nodded as Jack made a production out of swooping his black cape around her, granting her a searing kiss that melted away all the past hurts and made her go weak at the knees.

When the kiss was complete, she looked up into his eyes and said, "You're a changed man, Jack Peterson."

"Probably even more than you think," he chuckled. "I've decided to adopt Charlie too, and maybe a few more strays." He ran his hand under her hair, relishing its silky feel as he draped it over her shoulder.

Turning to the crowd, Jack waved his hands to get their attention. "I have two more surprises for you. First, *The Double Shot* is one-hundred percent animal-friendly. You'll find bowls of water and treats for your pets on the porch and next to the fireplace."

"Woohoo!" The crowd clapped and slapped one another on the back.

Jack raised his hands, trying to calm the revelers. When he had their attention again, he continued. "Also, when you enter *The Double Shot* and look to the right, you'll see an open archway leading into Decadent Desserts. That way, it's easier for you to enjoy the finest chocolates and confections this side of Pluto. Now, I'd like to welcome you all to *The Double Shot!*"

Jack swooped Lanie into his arms and carried her across the threshold.

Her eyes went wide when she saw the decorative archway leading into her shop.

"This way, we can see each other whenever we want," Jack said. "I can stare longingly at you, and you can treat me to those sexy dimples of yours. I promise you, baby, I'm never leaving you ever again, much less letting you out of my sight. I'm here to stay."

Melanie's heart raced as she wriggled out from his arms. "How Jack? When did you do all of this?" She bounded through the archway, her boots skidding to a halt in the middle of Decadent Desserts: At least a hundred Halloween arrangements of orange roses, tiger lilies, day lilies, and marigolds filled the shop, and a plush bed for Charlie was nestled beside the fireplace that now opened into both spaces.

"It's amazing what a man in love can accomplish these days," Jack said. He leaned against the edge of the brick fireplace and smiled, taking in the beauty and joy that was Melanie.

"It's breathtaking, Jack!" She tilted her head back, raised her arms to her sides, and twirled around. Sprinting toward the archway, she brushed her fingers along the artistic finish, then knelt to smell a bouquet of roses positioned by the fireplace. "I absolutely love it! I love everything you've done!" She raised herself up, opening her arms toward him. "And I love you."

Jack stepped into her embrace. "I love you too, Lanie. More than anything."

She wound her hands around his neck, pulling him toward her. "Come here, my dog-lovin' man. Slap another kiss on me."

EPILOGUE

Two Months Later

"For those who desire more of an American coffee flavor—in other words, *watered down*—we present the café Americano."

Melanie rolled her eyes at the Italian barista's description. She caught sight of Jack making his way across the café, two pumpkin-infused espressos in hand.

"This should be good," he said, setting the demitasse cups on the round table before them.

The Italian continued in his baritone voice. "It comes from a double shot of espresso pulled long, topped with up to eight ounces of hot water. So, essentially, a strong, bold coffee."

"What about iced coffee?" Melanie asked, prompting a grin from Jack.

"Don't bait him, baby," he said.

"But it's such fun to see him get so flustered about us 'Americans' and our uncivilized methods."

"You just wait." Jack winked his thick lashes at her. "I've got some uncivilized methods to show you later."

Melanie grinned. "So how do you think Ed and Ralph are doing with *The Double Shot?*"

"I think they're having the time of their lives. Ed texted me and said they made a special plaque to put over Charlie's bed by the fireplace. Speaking of fireplaces...." Jack waggled his eyebrows. "I think it's time we headed back to our room to start lesson two-oh-two of the *Jack Peterson School of Espresso.*"

She glanced down to the cups he had placed on the table. "But what about these drinks? Don't you want to see if you'd like to partake in this Italian delicacy? I mean, really. We are in Venice and all."

"The only delicacy I want to partake in is sitting in front of me, fully clothed. I prefer my delicacies to be 'au naturel.'"

She stretched under the table and swept her ankle along his thigh.

Jack grabbed her foot in one strong hand. "You'd better be able to run in these boots. Think I can catch you?"

Melanie craned her head to peer around the table at her favorite pair of Luccheses. "In these babies? Not a chance."

"What do I win if I do?"

"Anything you want," she said, drawing out the words.

"Anything?" Jack asked, raising one brow.

"Anything!" Melanie shrieked as she bolted from the table. She turned the corner toward the lobby and dodged a barista gripping a silver tray. Then she ran up the ornate staircase leading to their room overlooking the Grand Canal.

***

"It's pretty much what it says: iced coffee." Jack ran a cube of ice up Melanie's arm.

"Jack, that's cold!"

He tossed the cube into the fire blazing beside the bearskin rug. "Come here, baby. I'll keep you warm."

Melanie snuggled into his arms, feeling his body heat radiate all around her. "Talk espresso to me, hot shot."

"Well, you start with coffee and add ice cubes to it to make it cold and watery, then add a double shot of espresso. We start by trying to brew the coffee to be stronger than normal. Then we add spices or sugar and let those dissolve. After chilling it, we pour the liquid over ice and add espresso, then mix with either light milk or whole milk and add syrups to the customers' taste, such as chocolate..."

Melanie nuzzled into his neck.

"Or iced mocha..."

She ran her hand slowly down his shirt, unbuttoning it along the way.

"Or caramel. Or hazelnut." Jack sighed and leaned toward her, resting his forehead against hers. "You're killing me here. How am I supposed to finish the lesson?"

"I have faith in you. You're a professional." She winked at him and lightly ran her hand down his bare chest, circled his belly button, then headed south. "But you'd better talk fast."

"Finally, we have flavored espressos. As you can probably guess, these are the same espresso drinks I mentioned earlier, but we add flavored syrups during the process. For café mocha, you add chocolate syrup or powder to a latte and add steamed milk to it."

"Are we almost finished?" She unzipped his jeans and tugged on his briefs.

Jack shifted onto his elbow and flung a hand over his heart. "My dear, we baristas take our espresso *very* seriously. We are forever chasing what we call the 'God shot.'"

"What's that?" Melanie gripped him and began stroking.

"Ummm...the perfect shot of espresso?" Jack tried to concentrate, but his body had other ideas.

"Maybe I should take a taste."

"Oh, I think you should."

Melanie leaned away from Jack.

"Where are you going?"

"To take a taste." She smiled at him, wiggling her backside as she sashayed to the coffee table that held the two espressos Jack had ordered downstairs.

"Come back here, Laine. Don't drink a full one or you'll never get to sleep."

"Who wants to sleep when I have you around?" She flashed him her dimples. "By the way, what do I win for beating you back to the room?"

Jack reached into a basket resting beside the fireplace and withdrew a small box.

"Jack...." She walked back toward the fire and knelt beside him, the flames leaping in a dance behind her.

He couldn't take his eyes off her. "Lanie, you are so beautiful."

Jack opened the blue velvet box. Shimmers of light danced off the emerald-cut diamond nestled inside.

"How about you and me...forever." He shifted to one knee and took her warm hand in his. "Lanie, will you marry me and make me the happiest barista in the world?"

Melanie leaned forward and wrapped him in her arms, pressing her bare breasts against the warmth of his chest, then leaned back to run a finger across the cool diamond. She raised one eyebrow. "Does this mean I get all the espresso I want?"

He eased back and saw the sparkle in her eyes. "It means I'll give you all the espresso as well as anything else in the world you desire. Please say you'll be my wife."

"Yes, Jack. Yes!" She reached out to kiss his lips that tasted of mocha and sugar, then pulled him down to the rug on top of her.

"You've made me the happiest barista on the planet," Jack said, slipping the ring onto her finger.

"What can I say?" Melanie chuckled. "It's not every gal that gets a double shot at love."

RECIPE

CREEPY CAULDRONS
Original Recipe by Cadia Cox

Ingredients:

16 small two-bite brownies
1/3 cup vanilla frosting
2 tablespoons green ready-to-decorate icing
1 teaspoon fresh espresso (optional, but delicious!)
16 gummy worms, cut in half
16 gummy spaghettis, cut in various lengths
40 edible candy eyes
Additional edible decorations as desired (ghosts, pumpkins, etc.)
16 thin pretzel sticks
Pieces of thin black licorice laces cut to 3 inch lengths (optional)

Instructions:

*To form the cauldrons, hollow out each brownie with a small knife or spoon leaving about ¼ inch around the edges.

*In a separate bowl, mix the vanilla frosting and ready-to-decorate icing. Add the icing in small amounts to achieve the ghoulish shade of green you prefer.

*Add the espresso to the frosting mixture. Be sure not to add too much espresso as it thins the filling.

*Spoon the filling into each cauldron until the frosting is level with the top of each brownie.

*Decorate by adding gummy worms, gummy spaghettis, candy eyes, and any other edible decorations you'd like.

*Add a pretzel stick to each cauldron for the stirrer.

*Bend the licorice laces into the shape of a handle and insert one lace into the sides of each cauldron, or add as spider legs to the base of the cauldrons.

I tried this recipe as Melanie originally created it—with tabasco—and true to Jack's reaction, they were too hot to eat! It turns out that adding fresh espresso to the filling was the secret ingredient this recipe needed.

Makes sixteen Creepy Cauldrons to enjoy during the holiday. Happy Halloween!

MISTLETOE &

MACAROONS

A Coral Cove Christmas Romance

CADIA COX

Ten Story Books, LLC
Dallas, TX

For the East Texas Lake Retreat Ladies,

*Thanks for wrangling me into
writing romance!*

CHAPTER ONE

"You can't be serious. I won *what?*" Sophie Dawson's voice squeaked like the pleather chair she was grasping, her signature flip-flops clapping against the black and white checked floor as she hopped up and down. "Where did you say it was?" Clutching the phone, she transitioned from hopping and began pacing around her hair salon, the *Twirl & Curl.*

"What is it?" her best friend, Melanie Baker, asked, in for her bi-monthly auburn touch-up.

Sophie swatted away her bestie's inquiry. She raked a shaking hand through her blonde curls before grasping the hem of her favorite peace-sign t-shirt, exposing her pierced belly button perched a few inches above denim cutoffs that rode low on her hips.

"Okay. Alright. Yes, that's my address. Thanks so much, Mr. Romano." Sophie's grin threatened to split her face. "You want me to call you Lorenzo? Um, sure, Lorenzo." She fanned herself with her free hand, clinking the multitude of metal charm bracelets she wore together.

Melanie flopped back in her chair and laughed out loud, then covered her mouth.

"Okay. See you then. Bye." Sophie disconnected the call and her giggles carried throughout the lavender and pink themed salon she'd saved up eight years to open. "Mel, you'll never believe who that was."

"Lorenzo Romano?" Melanie drew out the syllables, rolling her 'r's and batting her eyelashes.

"Exactly!" Sophie skipped around in a circle, acting like a kid who'd won a trip to see Santa's workshop at the North Pole.

Betty Eldridge, their long ago first grade teacher, emerged from under a mass of heat lamps that resembled a spider with red suction cup feet. Her unkempt silver hair stuck out from multiple squares of aluminum foil. "He's only the most famous Italian on the planet," she sighed. "Honey, if you don't snag that hunk of hotness, I'm going to snatch him right up myself." She held out her fashion magazine. "Show Mel this eye candy."

Sophie trotted over and examined the image, pressed the glossy pages to her chest, then delivered the magazine to Melanie who let out a shrill whistle. "He *is* hot."

"He's the premier hairdresser on this chunk of rock," Sophie said. "Sets all the latest trends. He's a freakin' genius. And I'm going to meet him!" She twirled in a circle, then flopped into an empty salon chair.

"And he owns *Romano's Salon*," Addie Beecham, another of Sophie's regulars, added, raising her head from the hot pink rinsing bowl. The blue-gray haired senior waved her boney hand. "You talk about global warming! With his good looks, he's liable to melt what's remaining of the ice caps."

Sophie sighed. "Oh, my God, he is gorgeous, isn't he?"

Melanie sat up and looked at her friend in the mirror. "So what did you win?"

Everyone turned to Sophie as her cheeks reddened. "An all-expense paid trip to Alaska..." Then came the words with a tremble of excitement— "...with *him*!" She ran in place, pumping her arms and legs up and down fast like a boxer getting ready for a match. She flung her head back and laughed, filling the salon with her joy.

Her longtime patrons clapped and whooped louder than when the Coral Cove Cougars won the state football championship.

"Seriously?" Melanie asked. She spun around in the chair to face Sophie directly. "That's awesome! But how?"

"Remember that convention I went to last spring in Houston?" Sophie collapsed into the chair beside Melanie. "Well, I signed up for the *Romano's Salon* sweepstakes. Mr. Romano—I mean, *Lorenzo*—just told me he put on the sweepstakes to get the word out that he's looking to expand his salons into Alaska and thought the drawing might woo some stylists to go up there and work for him. I figured there's no way I'd ever win. You know me—I've never won anything in my life, much less a trip."

"Yeah, I know." Melanie chuckled and stroked the soft red fur of the dachshund that snuggled in her lap. Melanie's fiancé, Jack, had adopted Charlie, but the puppy had decided to adopt Melanie. "I have to admit, I can't imagine you in Alaska. It's so cold up there. You're a dyed-in-the-dirt Texan. Do you even own a sweater?"

"Of course I own a sweater." Sophie tapped a finger next to the edge of her glossy pink lips. "Unless I donated it. I'll have to check. Besides, how cold can it really be up there? I wish it were a trip to the Caribbean, or the equator for that matter, but a trip's a trip, and it's far, far away from the parade of boring bachelors I've been dating lately."

"So when do you leave?" Melanie asked.

Sophie's voice became quiet. "Next week."

Melanie swiped her phone to the calendar app, careful not to startle Charlie. "But...but that's the week before Christmas. You know how much you love celebrating Christmas in Coral Cove. What about your mistletoe?"

For years, one of Sophie's secret traditions was to hang a sprig of mistletoe near the fireplace the night before Christmas. When she was a kid, she'd dreamed of her prince charming riding up on his bright white stallion and proposing to her on one knee under the mistletoe. Sophie had only shared the dream with the one person whom she knew would never make fun of it—Melanie.

Her best friend continued. "And what about our macaroon bake-a-thon? Who's going to cook with me?"

"Who cares about macaroons?" Betty interrupted. "Sophie *has* to go." She gestured toward Sophie in the same way she had pointed to their A, B, C's on the blackboard two decades earlier. "Can you imagine? Sophie with a gorgeous Italian? It's just what she needs to teach these no-good, self-centered boys in town a good lesson. The girl needs a sexy diversion after all the heartache she's had this year in the love department. Maybe a nice Italian fling will warm her up on those cold Alaskan nights."

Sophie leaned back and grinned, crossing her slender legs and bouncing the top one at high speed. "That's right. Besides, I'll be back by Christmas Eve, just in time to make our chocolate peanut butter macaroons. And you can help me find some mistletoe to hang. Gotta give it a chance to work its magic." She suddenly waxed dreamy. "Wonder if they have any mistletoe way up in Alaska."

Melanie scratched her temple. "No idea, but you know who's up there?"

Sophie shook her curls back and forth.

"Cole."

"You mean Nicky's best man?" Sophie wrinkled her slender nose. "That stuck up, straight-laced corporate weasel?"

Melanie's twin sister, Cassandra, had recently married Nicholas Sterling who ran his family's homebuilding enterprise in Phoenix. At the wedding reception, Sophie and Cole had shared one searing, sultry kiss.

Sophie wrapped her arms around her waist as she resurrected the feel of Cole's soft, knowing lips dancing with hers, turning her knees to jelly. Then she remembered how he had crushed her heart by pronouncing the most electrifying kiss of her life to be a mistake—a bad judgement call—on his part.

"Yeah, his VP of Operations," Melanie continued. "Well, until he resigned from Sterling a few months back. Wonder if you'll see him."

"Lordy, I hope not," Sophie said, shucking off the thought of the kiss that left her wanting more until his heartless statement convinced her it would never work between a hairdresser and a corporate curmudgeon. If it weren't for the magical setting of the wedding, the kiss would never have happened in the first place. "Besides, except for Lorenzo, I'm swearing off men as of today. I'm done with all the lying, cheating, self-centered bastards." Sophie swiped her hands across each other, as if to dust away the remnants of her failed relationships. Crinkling her brow, she said, "And as for Cole, I'm not getting within a thousand miles of him, especially if there's mistletoe around. I don't want to take any chances. Alaska's a big state, but it's not big enough for the two of us."

***

Cole Masterson had been in Alaska for two months: Sixty of the longest, dullest, most frustrating days of his life.

"Cole, can you please bring me some warm cocoa?" his mother, Marilyn, asked. She had broken her hip in four places in October when she slipped on a patch of ice in the library parking lot, and she still couldn't get around on her own.

"Coming right up, Mom." Cole finished washing a dish he remembered from childhood and wondered how the fragile piece of ceramic had survived breakage longer than his mother. Laying it on a towel to dry, he crossed the tiny kitchenette to the pantry and retrieved a box of instant cocoa. *Why couldn't she have bought a house with a dishwasher?* His hands had resembled ripe prunes since the brutally cold day he'd arrived. He snatched a coffee mug that said "Wild Girls of the North" from a hook over the sink, filled it with water, and placed it in the microwave. At least his mother had let him buy her one appliance to make life easier.

The timer dinged, and he dumped the cocoa into the mug, stirring until the powder disappeared. Glancing toward his mom, he shook his head at the sight of her relaxing in her Archie Bunker thrift store recliner, a romance novel settled in her hands. Crossing the room, he placed the yellow mug on an end table next to a photo of his brother and his brood.

His mother's eyes settled on the image as she wrapped fragile fingers around the mug handle. "You should find yourself a nice girl and settle down, like Cameron."

Cole swallowed hard, pushing the tightness in his throat out of the way. *If I hear that one more time, I'm going to find a bear to irritate—it would be safer.* "Yes, Mom. I will one of these days."

"I need more grandchildren, and I need them before I can't chase them around the yard anymore. One more fall like the one I just had and it might be my last. And I wouldn't get to see any of *your* children." She sniffled for effect, a tear creeping from the side of her eye.

Oh, great. Now she's crying on demand. "Yes, Mom. I know."

"I think tonight's ladies' night down at *The Purple Moose*." She cut her eyes toward Cole. Recent new strands of silver mingled with her natural brunette waves, brushing atop her narrow shoulders. "Maybe you could go into town and meet some of the local girls. Who knows, you might find 'The One.'"

Cole clenched his hands as he tried to control his temper that begged to be let loose. He didn't want a girlfriend, much less a wife—not with his history. "I don't think Hardly, Alaska is the place for me to meet 'The One.'"

His mother blew steam away from her cocoa, then took a small sip, licking the remnants from her lips. "You never know, dear." She set the mug on a coaster with a drawing of a musk ox on it. "You have to quit being so pessimistic."

"I'm not pessimistic, just realistic." His words sounded choppy and affronted, even to him.

"Then realistically speaking, I insist you go to *The Purple Moose* tonight. I promise I can fend for myself."

Cole let out a breath and reigned in his frustration. He was tired of this constant battle. "Look Mom, I didn't quit my job and come here to find a wife, or even a girlfriend for that matter. I came here to nurse you back to health." Grabbing a box of Ritz crackers from the counter, he opened the package and set it next to her cocoa, needing to do something—*anything*—other than have this discussion for the twenty-thousandth time.

"I know that, Cole, but I just want you to go out and have some fun." His mother waggled her brows and cocked her head toward him. "Loosen up that tie of yours."

He glanced down. "I'm not wearing a tie."

She looked heavenward and with a shuddering sigh, she turned toward her son. "That was just a figure of speech, Cole. Must you take everything so literally?"

Cole felt his cortisol levels rising with the frustration he couldn't seem to overcome. Maybe a night out of the house would be good for him. "Fine. I'll go out after I finish the dishes."

"Leave those pesky dishes," she said, flinging her wrists toward the kitchenette. "They'll be here when you get back. And Cole? Put on one of your dad's old flannel shirts and jeans I kept, you know, so you won't look like you just stepped out of the city."

Cole glanced down to his wool-blend slacks and dress shirt that he considered casual. "But I like my clothes."

"I know you do, son. I'm just looking out for you. These Alaskan girls may think you're a metrosexual or something."

He really needed to escape from this excuse for civilization before he went mad.

CHAPTER TWO

Frigid Alaskan air assaulted Sophie's bare toes as she stepped out of the puddle jumper and planted her flip-flops on the tarmac of the Hardly, Alaska International Airport.

Okay, so maybe it can get pretty dang cold up here. I should've listened to Mel and bought some wintery clothes. And warmer shoes, she thought, as one flip-flop slid off her foot, landing her toes in icy slush.

"Dang, this stuff's cold," she clipped, shaking her foot, then slipping her favorite Haviana back on. She quickly realized Melanie was right—her signature t-shirts and thin cotton leggings might be fine in a Texas Gulf Coast cold snap, but they were no match for the wind whipping off the ice-covered lake that bordered the airport.

Glancing behind her, she watched enviously as the pilot and lone flight attendant disappeared into puffy coats and gloves before descending the plane's stairs. Turning back toward the terminal, or what might pass for a single person hut, she wondered how anyone could choose to live in this desolate, frozen wasteland. Every inch of the ground was white, including the runway. Luckily the plane hadn't slid down the tarmac when they'd landed. She shivered and added a pair of fuzzy boots to her mental shopping list before leaning down to grab her two bags, only to have a gloved hand descend on top of hers.

"My sweet biscotti, you mustn't burden your delicate hands with such things." The syllables slipped off the owner's tongue like silk sheets off a mattress.

"Lorenzo, you really must let me carry my own bags." Sophie tried to jerk the luggage back toward her.

The short-statured Italian shook his long, impeccably formed curls until they draped behind his broad shoulders. "Miss Sophia, it is my pleasure beyond words for me to escort you on this trip to the great northern state of Alaska. Please, my darling, my honey bee, I will carry your bags for you and buzz behind your every footstep."

Sophie squeezed her toes together, begging the weather to magically warm up before they were overcome with frostbite. "No, Lorenzo, honestly...I can get my own bags."

"I am smitten by your beauty, Miss Sophia. How ever am I going to be able to still my heart that beats like a drum, sounding across the barren plains of my existence?" He reached for her hand, caressing her skin with his thumb. "And we must get some warm shoes for your delicate feet before the snow freezes your tenderest toes."

"Lorenzo...." Sophie squeezed her eyes shut and tried to figure out how to stop him from coming on to her. He had been courting her since the moment he sat down beside her in first class. Being famous wasn't something she had ever placed in high regard, and although he'd long been her idol, she soon figured out she had no desire to be his honey bee.

"We are, how do you say it—'stuck at the hips'—for our time in theez winter wonderland, theez desert of snow that looks like a cotton machine blew up."

Sophie couldn't help but laugh at his attempt to speak a language that was as native to him as Swahili was to her. "Let's just rent a car and get to the hotel."

"Your wish is my happiness," Lorenzo said, holding his hand up to his heart. "I do believe I am falling in love with you, Miss Sophia. Perhaps we must share the body heat to stay warm together?" He raised his manicured eyebrows, then huddled close to her side, slipping a brave arm around her waist.

"It's Sophie," she said, grabbing his wrist and separating it from her body. "And there's no way you could be in love with me." She lifted her bags and marched, flip-flops flapping, toward the lone car parked in the lot. "We've only known each other for ten hours, tops. And besides...." She stopped, turned to face him, and breathed in the frigid air. *Go ahead, you can do this. If you don't, you're going to have to fight him off all week.* "I'm engaged."

Lorenzo's face turned ashen as he collapsed against the terminal hut, clutching his chest.

"But it can't be, mio amore."

"Yes, it can."

He lifted her left hand. "But what is this? You have no ring?"

Sophie wriggled her hand free. "He's looking for the perfect one to match my—" *My what? My what?* "My eyes." *Oh, great; brilliant answer.*

"I do not believe you." Lorenzo crossed his stubby arms and tapped a designer loafer in the snow, then squinted his amber eyes. "What is this man's name, the one who has captured your heart?"

"His name?" Sophie's voice squeaked.

"Yes, my peach parfait. His name." A sultry smile nudged Lorenzo's prominent cheekbones.

Fine, now you've got to come up with a fake fiancé. Think, girl. Think. Sophie grabbed at the first name that leapt into her mind. "Cole. It's Cole Masterson. He...um...he lives up here."

Lorenzo's laughter tumbled through the air. "You are a very funny lady, my Sophia." He strummed the side of her cheek with the cool tips of his fingers. "You are playing the hards to get." He smiled at her and patted her shoulder. "But I am in love with you, my creamy cannoli. I shall fight for you against this supposed 'fiancé.'"

Sophie let out a deep breath and watched it form into a cloud in front of her. "There is no way you can be in love with me, Lorenzo. We just met."

"Ah, yes, but love is timeless. It can happen like theez." He snapped his fingers so hard that his shiny brown ringlets bounced against his colorful knit sweater.

Sophie approached the car and found a note on the dash: *If you need Bessie, take her and return her whenever you want. Keys are in the ignition.*

"Come on, Romeo. Let's get going."

"It is Romano, my sweet candy blossom." He maneuvered past Sophie and strode toward the car. "And I will chauffer you in Bessie during our winter adventure in this great white north."

Sophie snorted. *That's what you think.*

***

The Purple Moose. Cole walked through the narrow door and stumbled back as he inhaled a gulp of smoke swirling through the bar tucked inside the town's only hotel. Television sets kept patrons enthralled with football games from the lower forty-eight, cheers and boos erupting with every play.

Great. This is Hardly's primo bar?

"What can I get ya?" The barkeep tossed a towel across his shoulder. At about five-foot-eight, he was shorter than Cole by a good six inches, but he won out in the weight contest. He had to be at least two-fifty, as opposed to Cole's slender, yet fit six-two frame.

Cole shifted onto a leather barstool and studied the chalk menu above the mirror behind the bar. "I'll have a scotch, neat."

The bartender lifted one side of his lips in a friendly smile, then poured two fingers for Cole. Sliding the glass toward him, he said, "Haven't seen you 'round here before."

Cole chuckled. "Yeah, well, I'll be here for a while. Helping my mom after she broke her hip."

The bartender leaned against the dull wood bar and dried a beer mug. "You mean Miss Marilyn up on the hill? You're her kid?"

Cole raised his shoulders and smirked. "Guilty, as charged." He extended his hand. "Cole Masterson."

The barkeep wiped his hand and shook Cole's. "I'm Buddy. Your mom's a great lady. Looks good for her age. Man, oh man, if I was twenty years younger...."

Cole raised his hand and cut him off, lowering his head and shaking it. "Please don't go there. That's my mother you're talking about."

"Na, I'm talking about that beaut' walkin' your way. Whooeee...."

Cole felt himself being grabbed by the shoulders, swung around, and flung backward toward the bar. A woman lunged at him, clinging to him like a toddler to a candy bar and then started kissing him like he was the last man in Alaska.

These Alaskan women really don't waste time.

He felt warm, smooth lips trail along his jaw and move up toward his ear. Muscles he had long forgotten quivered at the sultry kisses, kisses that reminded him of....

No. It can't be.

Placing his hands on the woman's soft shoulders, he turned to view his attacker and his heart tumbled in his chest.

Sophie.

He'd recognize that particular flower child anywhere.

What's she doing here? She doesn't even own a heavy coat, much less gear to be here in the winter.

He stared straight at her as their eyes met.

She leaned close, kissed him on his earlobe, and whispered, "Play along, Cole. Please." She shifted back and exclaimed, "Darling!"

He jerked at her shrill voice, then felt a solid tap on his shoulder.

"You—*you* are the supposed 'fiancé' of my buttercup?" A short, stocky silhouette attempted—and failed—to tower over him.

"The what of your what?" Cole scratched his chin and stared at the man with ringlets who looked as out of place as a Chihuahua on Mount Everest.

"That's right," Sophie said, stroking her hand down Cole's cheek and wrapping her arms around his neck which had flipped into sensitivity overdrive. "This is Cole. My fiancé."

Cole flinched at the word, but Sophie held him in place. She turned to look at the man behind her who seethed as if a bully had stolen his favorite toy. Sophie shifted and met Cole's eyes with a quick wink. "I've missed you so much, baby," she purred.

"Cole." The word dripped off the man's lips with a touch of turpentine. "My name is Lorenzo. Lorenzo Romano. And I challenge you to a duel to win the hand of Miss Sophia." He raised a finger in the air to emphasize his call to duty.

Cole laughed as he looked down at the man who, on a good day, might have stretched to five-foot-four. "A duel? I don't know about that." He felt sharp fingernails dig into his forearm through his dad's old shirt.

"You'd be willing to fight for me, wouldn't you, darling?" Sophie batted her lashes at him over a stare that could slay vampires.

"It depends," Cole said, lifting an elbow to rest against the bar. "We aren't talking a duel to the death or anything?"

A laugh rolled out of Lorenzo's throat. "We shall see who my sugar cookie chooses before this week is over." He leaned toward the bar. "Sauvignon blanc, per favore."

Sophie grabbed the glass from Cole's hand and downed his scotch in one swallow, cringing for a second as the sharp liquid burned its way down her throat.

"Yes," Cole said, getting a little too comfortable having Sophie's arms around him. "We'll see."

CHAPTER THREE

Cole had thought the drive back home from the bar would give him time to come to his senses. But all he could think about was the feel of Sophie's breath on his cheek, the heat from her hands burning through his shirt, and the taste of his scotch mingling with her seductive lips.

"Cole? Is that you?" His mother's voice called out from the cozy family room.

"Yes, it's me." His reply threatened to choke him. He cleared his throat, trying to dislodge the guilt that had taken up residence there. "And I, um, have a surprise for you."

"You do?" Excitement laced her voice, with a touch of concern.

"Yes. I'll be there in a second." Cole turned to Sophie. "Remember, you promised you'd make this look good."

Sophie wound her hands around his arm, raised on her tiptoes, and whispered in his ear. "But we're deceiving your—your *mother*. Isn't that a sin or something?" She scrunched her eyebrows together and cocked her head.

"No more than the sin of lying to lover boy over there." He motioned toward the snow-dusted driveway where his truck dwarfed the compact car Lorenzo disagreeably warmed himself in while sulking. "Besides, you're actually doing me a favor. This'll get her off my back for a while about getting married and giving her grandkids."

Lorenzo preened his hair in the back seat of the car, then looked at Sophie with sad, puppy dog eyes.

Cole stepped from behind the door and pulled Sophie along. "Come on. He's fine out there. He's a grown man."

"But he looks so, I don't know, forlorn."

Cole ignored her concern. "Mom, I'd like you to meet someone." He gripped Sophie's hand like he was squeezing a stress ball, but he loosened it when he heard a small whimper escape her throat. They stepped into the family room together. "This is Sophie. My...fiancée." He placed a stiff arm around Sophie's shoulder. "Sophie, this is my mom, Marilyn Masterson."

Confusion crossed his mother's eyes. She looked at Sophie, glancing up and down, then her slight grin turned into a full wattage smile. "Well, my dear, it's a pleasure to meet you." She clasped her hands together and glared at Cole. "My, my, this is sudden. Um, how did you two meet?"

"In Coral Cove," they both said, smiling at each other, proud that they'd practiced a few basic questions on the walk up the driveway. The rules of their ploy were still in discussion, but they had agreed on the major points: no public displays of affection more than chaste cheek kisses and an occasional light hug; no sleeping in the same room, much less the same bed; and absolutely no sex.

Sophie wanted to argue the last point, just to make him angry. At Cassandra's wedding, they'd argued about everything from the music selection to the choice of entrees. Come to think of it, arguing with Cole had been the most fun part of the nuptials for her. But she knew when to let a topic go, so after he had dispersed his set of rules for this ruse, she'd informed Cole she was never getting married—that she'd given up on men in general—so that should be enough to assure him she wasn't interested in his magnetic good looks and all the heartbreak that came with dating winners of the DNA lottery.

"Why haven't I heard about you before?" Marilyn asked. "And my dear, where is your ring?" Turning toward her son, she said, "Every girl needs a ring. A nice, big, fat diamond ring."

Sophie flounced over to the sofa, plopped down beside the older woman, and enveloped her in a hug.

"I'm getting to it," Cole said, berating himself for overlooking the significant detail. "I haven't found the right one for her yet."

"I think it's because Cole is still trying to wrap his conservative mind around the fact that he fell for such a free spirit. Isn't that right, honey?" Sophie nudged a curl away from her cheek and drew her now bare feet up under her like a child ready for story time.

Cole rolled his eyes. "Yeah, that's it. Look, Mom, I need to get Sophie back to the hotel, but I wanted to introduce you to her first."

"Scusi. And what about me?" Lorenzo appeared in the doorway, then swooshed around Cole and knelt in front of Sophie and Marilyn, grabbing one hand from each and planting a kiss on them. "What am I? The sliced gizzards?"

"And this is?" Marilyn's eyes twinkled as she raised her brows.

"Signora, I am Lorenzo Romano, in the flesh and the bones." Lorenzo bowed his head, then flipped his curls to settle them along his shoulders. "I am not convinced it is true love between my sweet strudel and..." He cocked his head toward Cole and growled, "...*heem.*"

Cole gripped the back of the closest chair, a groan escaping his reserve. "Mom, Sophie's a hairdresser in

Coral Cove. She's best friends with Nicholas's wife's twin sister, Melanie. She won this trip to Alaska from Lorenzo's stylist company, and we thought it would be a good time for her to come meet you. You *do* want grandkids before you fall again, don't you?"

"Mmm hmm," his mother hummed, her eyes shifting between the two of them, then a twinkle emerged. "Why don't you all stay for dinner? Cole can cook a mean pot roast."

"Oh, no. No way. Not in this lifetime." Sophie clenched her hands around her stomach and looked queasy. "I'm a vegetarian."

"What is this vegemama?" Lorenzo asked.

"No, I said 'vegetarian.'" Sophie drew her knees up to her chest and covered them with an animal print throw tossed across the back of the sofa. "You know; I don't eat meat."

Lorenzo cocked his head like a confused cocker spaniel. "But my sugar blossom, why would you do a crazy thing like that? A life without meat? Without...zee bacon?"

Sophie shivered and shook her head. "Yuck. It's because I believe in animal rights, and I don't want any precious creatures hurt. And eating them, well, that's just disgusting."

"Come on, now," Cole said, rubbing Sophie's back. "You know Mom and Dad were cattle ranchers when Dad was alive. I'm...we're all meat-eaters."

"Well, I'm not, and I don't think you should be either." She patted his belly. "The fat is really bad for you. If you keep eating it, you'll make me an early widow." She shivered and withdrew her hand, immediately feeling the loss of connection with her new fiancé. "I'm too young for that. Besides, I'd have to wear black, and it's such a dreary color."

"Soph," Cole growled.

"Sorry big guy, but I can't. I won't." She jerked her head toward Marilyn, dismissing Cole.

Marilyn laughed and leaned toward Lorenzo who had claimed the spot on the other side of her. "This should be interesting. Very interesting."

***

Cole pulled Sophie into the kitchenette and lowered his voice so his mom and Lorenzo couldn't hear them. "How can you be from cattle country and not eat meat?"

"It's easy." Sophie opened the tiny refrigerator and perused the offerings. "I just look at the plate, and if it's leafy and green, it makes me happy. If it once had a face, it makes me sad."

Cole smirked. "Then you're going to be sad a lot around here."

"Seriously, Cole?" She stood tall in an attempt to try and meet him eye level, but looked dejected when she realized the futility. "Can't you forego meat just until the end of the week?" The begging in her voice almost made him give in. Almost.

"Mom is never going to buy that you are my soulmate. Not if you won't eat meat." He pulled a container of raw vegetables out of the fridge along with a package of raw meat.

"Well, you can put it on my plate, but I won't touch it. And I have to warn you: I might throw-up." Fake-retching, she leaned over the sink and coughed.

"Fine," Cole said. "I'll try, but I insist on having one last meaty meal tonight. You're going to have to do a lot of good acting on your part if I have to give up my morning bacon."

They prepared dinner side by side while they listened to Lorenzo and Marilyn's laughs drifting across the house like the scent of freshly baked cookies.

"Looks like those two are getting along." Sophie nudged her head toward the pair who bantered like old friends. She rinsed a head of lettuce, then laid it on the cutting board, sliced it into small pieces, and tossed it into a large bamboo bowl.

"Yeah. Looks that way." Cole pursed his lips and handed her two peeled carrots, a zucchini, and an onion, then peered around his shoulder and growled.

Sophie chopped and diced the colorful vegetables and added them to the salad, then poured oil and vinegar into a small pot and combined it with a teaspoon of Dijon mustard and a shake of sea salt and black pepper.

"Here, add some of this." Cole handed Sophie a glass jar.

"Peanut butter? I love peanut butter." She scooped a spoonful and added it to the dressing, mixing it until it was smooth.

"That's probably the only thing in this world we agree on," Cole said, throwing a couple of steaks into a pan on the stove. The meat sizzled the moment it hit the hot surface.

Sophie's eyes grew large as she saw drips of blood dotted across the Formica counter. "That's it, Cole." She threw her spatula toward the sink and untied the apron she'd found in the towel drawer. "I'm going to the hotel."

"Soph, you can't," Cole said. "You have to eat here or Mom won't believe we're an item."

"If we keep fighting like this, we won't be an item much longer." She marched to the pantry where she'd left her flip-flops and slid them on.

Cole huffed. "Fine. I'll give up meat for a few days. But would you please at least put on some real clothes? Something that's not so revealing? No wonder lover boy over there can't keep his hands off you."

She glanced at her fitted *Save the Whales* tank top and navy leggings, twisting to review her attire from multiple angles. Raising her eyes toward his gold-flecked pair, she lifted one side of her lips into a smirk and placed her hands on her hips. "Are you jealous? Is that why you're so testosterony?"

"Me? Jealous? Of you and *him?*" Cole pointed toward Lorenzo and shook his head at the crazy notion. "How insulting. For the last time—I'm not interested in a relationship with *anyone*. I have one goal, and one goal only: to get my mom healed so I can try and salvage my career."

"Everything has to be nice and orderly for you, doesn't it?" She pulled a can of beans from the shelf and slammed it on the counter. "You can't take things as they come."

"That's right. I've already had to give up my job to be here." Cole hated arguing, especially with someone who argued back.

"I'm sure Nicky will give you your job back. He's a gentleman, unlike *some* males in this room."

"Maybe, but I can't count on it. The only other thing I was good at years ago was working the *Rocking M*—our family ranch. But I don't plan on going back to Texas. If I did, I guess I could be a rancher again."

"With cows?" Sophie asked.

"Yes."

"And chickens?"

"Yeah."

"For milk and eggs, or meat and meat?"

"All of the above."

"Well," she said. "I can tell you one thing. We will *never* make it with *that* kind of attitude."

CHAPTER FOUR

Dim rays of sunlight crept across the horizon as morning fought to make an appearance. The winter months made parts of Alaska dark twenty-four seven, but Hardly was far enough south to catch a few hours of the lazy sun.

Sophie and Lorenzo's hotel, *The Tickled Marlin*, was nestled between the Hardly Hungry grocery store and the Hardly Full general store. Sophie studied the quirky décor in the nautical-themed hotel, from the record-breaking swordfish decorated with tinsel and garland to the stuffed eight-foot Grizzly hovering beside the revolving door with a salmon clenched in its mouth and a Santa hat perched on its head. Although Marilyn had offered the evening before to let Sophie and Lorenzo stay with her and Cole, it had been apparent there would not be enough room for four people in the small home, much less two feuding Type-A males.

Sophie's pulse rose when she saw Cole stride toward the hotel door in a worn pair of jeans that fit snug against his shapely thighs and an ass that should be starring in TV underwear ads. Her breath hitched as he raised his arm to thrust open the door.

Don't let his drop-dead body make you weak, girl. He may be as tempting as a slice of home-made lemon merengue pie, but....

"Mornin'," Cole said, his Texas drawl inching through the city slicker façade he liked to wear.

"Um," Sophie felt her knees go weak as she swayed toward him. Cowboy accents did that to her. Always had.

"Whoa, there." He grasped her arms, as though he were steadying a princess. Tipping back his dad's felt Stetson, his gold eyes searched her blue ones. "You okay?"

Sophie felt dizzy, like she had just ridden the Tea Cups at Disneyland. Pulling her chin up, she looked into his mesmerizing eyes as everything around them turned fuzzy, just like in the movies. "Yeah, I'm fine," she whispered.

"There you are, my blueberry muffin."

Lorenzo's term of endearment sliced through Sophie's unexpected connection to Cole. She tried to grasp at it again, but the moment was over.

"I have with me a list of fun Alaska-y things that will make my raspberry tart want to be mine forever." Lorenzo stared at Sophie, then Cole, then back toward

Sophie. He thrust a manicured finger into the air and pointed it. "Is *he* coming with us?"

"Yes," Cole said, as Sophie said, "No."

Cole shook his head. "I cannot in good conscience let you two traipse around Alaska in Bessie. You'll disappear in a snowdrift as fast as a prairie dog darts underground. Then you wouldn't be found until the spring thaw."

Lorenzo's pale skin became paler, if that was even possible. "You mean—we could freeze? To the *deaths?*"

"It's a definite possibility." Cole tightened his lips, then let a grin slide past before reeling in his sarcastic attitude.

"Then si, you may be our chauffeur, mountain man. Besides, I do not have a license to drive, and I do not like my little buttercup having to drive in this, this slush." He waved his hand toward the snow drifts standing sentinel near the hotel door.

"For the umpteenth time, I am *not* your little buttercup. My name is Sophie." She stomped her new fleece-lined boots she'd purchased at the general store. Nestling into her new insulated coat, courtesy of the general store as well, she pulled her also new knit cap down over her ears and marched out the door toward Cole's dirty truck. She blew out a breath. "You could have at least washed it for us."

"No need in this muck. It won't be cleaned until spring." Cole grasped Sophie's arm to steady her.

"Keep your filthy hooves off my—"

A crash sounded behind them as they heard a screeching yelp. Turning toward the pitiful sound, they saw Lorenzo lying flat on a patch of ice like a crime scene outline staring at the overcast sky.

Sophie drew her new mittens to her mouth. "Lorenzo, are you okay?" She tiptoed toward the downed hairdresser.

Lorenzo rubbed his hip and grabbed for his ankle. "Oh, my crème-filled bonbon, I believe I have twisted my ankle. Owww...." He screeched like a barn owl.

"Stay put," Cole told Sophie. "I don't want you to fall, too. I'll take care of Casanova." He marched toward the whimpering man and knelt to examine the sprain. Unwrapping the gray scarf from his neck, he filled it with snow and secured it around Lorenzo's ankle.

"Ow! Oh the cold!" Lorenzo cried out. "You are a mean man. A very mean man. Are you trying to give me the early deaths?" He spewed off several Italian phrases that didn't sound like they would be appropriate for mixed company if translated into English.

Cole shifted to stand above Lorenzo. "Just trying to keep the swelling down." He extended his hand.

Lorenzo sneered at Cole's leather glove, but allowed him to pull him up. He swung his arm over Cole's shoulder. "I cannot take this ice and snow prison anymore. It makes my nose drip waters and my eyes sting like the needles."

Cole took a step forward, but stopped when Lorenzo squealed in his ear.

"Oh, the pain, the pain!"

Sophie laid her hand on Lorenzo's arm. "Are you okay? Did you hurt your cutting hand?"

"Ah, my delicate baklava, your concern heals my heart." He smiled at her and smirked at Cole. "But I feel I must stay inside today and warm my fingers. They are insured, but I so detest dealing with the insurance people. They ask too many questions of me. Maybe I should rethink opening a *Romano's Salon* in this—this icy land where you can see every breath you take." He blew air from his mouth, then held out his hands and stretched his fingers as if trimming someone's hair in the fog he'd created. "Would you be heart-cracked if I didn't go to see the running doggies with you, my candy confection?"

"Of course not," Sophie said. "You have to keep your hands safe. What would the world do without your trend-setting styles?"

Sophie situated herself under Lorenzo's other arm and helped Cole turn him back toward the hotel.

"No," Lorenzo cried out. "Do not leave me in this place of cold rooms and tiny drinks. I will go to Miss Marilyn's house and sit by the fire with her and warm myself with brandy. Cole, would you please escort me to her house and then take my peach pudding to see the doggies? And then to the other surprise places on my list?" He held out a folded piece of paper.

Cole looked from Lorenzo to Sophie and caught the slight hitch in her breath. "I'd be happy to," he said, grabbing the itinerary.

"But mister Alaska, no kissing my sugar dumpling. We still must duel for her." He massaged his fingers, checking the integrity of each one like he was a hand model before a photo shoot, then slipped them into his coat pockets. "And I must heal before I can fight."

"Of course," Cole said. He helped lift Lorenzo into the back seat of the truck. "I'll make sure she sees every sight you have planned."

"I thank you, mister mountain man, from the bottom of my lungs," Lorenzo said. "I must say, I do look forward to learning the secret of Miss Marilyn's silky hair."

"You keep your insured fingers out of my mom's hair," Cole warned him, pointing his index finger toward Lorenzo's face.

Sophie turned from the front seat and crinkled her brow. "Are you sure you don't want me to stay with you, Lorenzo? I feel terrible you're hurt."

"I am not in too much pain now, my sugar plum, but I promised for you to see the Alaskan sights. After my accident, I am only in need of Miss Marilyn's cocoa and a respite from this world carpeted in white and wrapped in coldness." Lorenzo shivered, then straightened his back and faced Cole. "And mister sticky fingers, you must keep my cherry cupcake safe from avalanches. I have seen on the television what can happen when your snow collapses on fair maidens. And above all, you must vow to keep your hands off of my delicate Sophia."

"Sophie!" Cole and Sophie yelled together.

Turning to scan the horizon, Cole said, "I can assure you she's safe with me."

That's what you think, Sophie thought, her girlie muscles tightening at the sound of Cole's authoritative voice. Her hands became clammy inside her thick mittens, and her heart began betraying her vow to give up all men.

***

Cole watched Sophie nuzzle her face into the Alaskan husky's thick fur and jolted at the thought he was jealous of a dog.

"I've never felt fur so soft in my life," Sophie said, her face beaming as she looked up at Cole. "Feel this fella's coat."

Cole reached down and patted the gray dog behind its ears. "Definitely soft," he said, gazing into Sophie's eyes. He longed to run his hands through her silky, sun-kissed blonde hair and continue down her body, pulling aside her panties to see for himself if it was indeed her natural color.

Nothing about Alaska was going how he had planned: not his mother's recovery, and as frustrating as he found her spontaneity, not his feelings for this carefree woman beside him. His best friend and former employer, Nicholas, had tried to set him up with Sophie at his wedding. But after one hotter-than-hell kiss that jolted him like a California quake, the decade-old guilt that plagued Cole refused to let him have anything to do with the flighty hairdresser who lived in tie-dye shirts, barely-there cut-offs, and daisy-embellished flip-flops. She was his complete opposite and as different from the professional, goal-oriented women he dated as whiskey was from water. But the memory of that one searing kiss they'd shared came roaring back. Was that why he couldn't take his eyes off her?

"Would you like to meet the whole team?" Grace Lombardi, the sled dog team owner, motioned toward the barn. Her tall frame towered over Sophie, but the gruff woman didn't intimidate her.

"Of course," Sophie said, springing to her feet, eliciting a bark from her new best friend. "Can Zeus come with us?"

Grace nodded and began walking. "He'll come whether we want him to or not. Comes with being the lead dog."

Cole watched the women as they chatted like old friends and followed them to the kennels.

"Sled dog teams, like mine, that run the Iditarod are northern breeds, which means they have a natural fur layer that keeps them warm," Grace said. "They're mostly called Alaskan huskies."

Sophie crinkled her nose. "Don't their little paws get cold?"

Grace shook her head and smiled. "They're like my kids—I wouldn't let them go out without being protected. They each have light jackets to keep them warm during the race, but not so warm they overheat. They even have windbreakers, just like we wear." She petted each dog, letting Sophie feed them treats as they went.

Grace reached inside her pocket and withdrew a set of keys. "I need to head north to pick up some supplies while the weather's good, but feel free to walk around the kennels and play with any of the dogs you'd like." She tossed the keys to Cole. "Just lock up when you're done if you don't mind. I've known Marilyn ever since she moved up here, and I've seen Cole with the dogs and trust him to show you around. With you two being engaged and all, you're practically family now."

A flush of guilt rushed up Sophie's cheeks.

"Thanks, Grace," Cole said, wrapping his arm around Sophie's waist. "We'll be careful with them and check the locks when we leave." Heat emanated from underneath Sophie's sweater, burning his hand like he'd brushed against fresh lava.

A whimper wafted up from the corner of the barn, and Sophie went to investigate.

"Well, who do we have here?" she said, kneeling beside a bale of hay. "Looks like you're stuck."

"That's Sleigh Belle," Cole said, reaching down to dislodge the pint-sized pup from a tangled towel. "She's the runt of Grace's latest litter."

"How can anyone call this cute little gal a runt?" Sophie's features softened as she reached out to pet the bouncing puppy.

Sleigh Belle's charcoal-tipped ears stood at attention above her rounded face. Her short tail rotated like a propeller, and her feet danced on the ground, eager to jump up and smother Sophie with kisses.

"She's not that much smaller than the others," Cole said. "But Grace says she's too playful and small to be a race dog."

Sophie reached toward Cole and took the puppy in her arms. "Well, I think she's perfect."

Cole's heart thudded in his chest as he watched her stroke the soft fur atop the pup's head. Once again, he was jealous of a canine.

CHAPTER FIVE

"What's the deal with the Iditarod?" Sophie raised her head from snuggling with Sleigh Belle and faced Cole. "I know it's a famous race and all, but I don't know much about it."

Cole motioned to a couple of chairs by a stack of blankets. "Let's sit down and I'll see what I can remember from what Grace has told me before."

Sophie lowered herself into a blue director's chair with Zeus's name embroidered in gold thread on the fabric. She placed Sleigh Belle in her lap, allowing the pup to march in circles until she found the perfect spot to lie down. She stroked the fluffy, uneven tufts of hair on the tiny pup's head as she turned to listen to Cole.

Think about the race, dude. Forget about what her hands would feel like stroking you. You can't go there, not with her. Not with anyone. He swallowed hard, then tried to imagine being outside naked, rolling in the snow to cool off the desire burning in him like a forest fire. He felt himself being drawn into her spell, but he couldn't go there. Sophie was the marrying type, whether she knew it or not. And he wasn't. He certainly wasn't a saint, but he'd never shared his bed for more than two or three months with any woman. And they'd always known up front he wasn't a long-term kind of guy. He couldn't be. Not after what he'd done.

Cole shifted to accommodate the growing tightness in his pants. "The race is just over a thousand miles. It's run each year from Anchorage to Nome, through what Grace swears is some of the most gorgeous terrain in the world. She says it skirts jagged mountains and crosses everything from tundra to frozen rivers, then juts up against the coastline. The temps go way below zero, and the wind gets so intense that teams can be in a white-out just like that." He snapped his fingers. "Another of Alaska's extremes."

Cole brushed against Sophie's leg as he reached over to pet Sleigh Belle. Her voice hitched at the touch, making him think he might have a chance. But did he want one? Could he want one?

"How can these precious animals survive?" Sophie asked, her voice shaky. "I mean, I almost became a popsicle when I stepped off the plane and my flip-flop fell off in the snow."

Cole slanted his head toward her and smirked. "But you had lover boy to keep you warm."

"Yes, Lorenzo," she said. "I'd almost forgotten about him. I don't think there was enough alcohol on that plane to dull my frustration with his wooing efforts. I swear, he can be relentless. Thanks again for playing the fiancé part."

Cole's stomach clenched as realization struck him: he had become used to thinking of her as his fiancée. And worse: he liked it. He felt a connection to Sophie, unlike any he'd ever experienced. She wasn't after his money, and she seemed to honestly like him as a person. She'd awakened a part of him that had long been imprisoned, the part that wanted the whole package: the white picket fence, the two kids—and a sled dog. The whole package he could never allow himself to have.

Shaking off the ridiculous notion and attempting to separate himself from his growing lust, he shifted his thoughts back to the race. "Iditarod means 'distant place' in the natives' language up here. The whole thing started when, during the gold rush days, they needed to get mail to Iditarod and other remote places. And they needed to get the gold out during the height of the rush. Back then, sled dog teams made it all happen."

"Your ancestors were quite the life-savers," Sophie said to Sleigh Belle. The pup squirmed in her lap, then curled against Sophie's belly.

Oh God, Cole thought, silently begging her to quench his desire, to wrap him in her arms, to take him deep inside and save *his* life. Cole's voice cracked. "Yeah.

Literally life-savers." *Christ, I've got to stop wanting her to pet me like that.*

Cole cleared his throat. His head spun from the growing hunger for her body. And her soul. If she would only rhythmically stroke him like she was stroking the puppy, maybe his libido could be satiated and set him free from this ravenous need he was barely holding under control.

He forced his tongue to form coherent words. "The worst time was probably when the diphtheria epidemic threatened Nome. They needed serum, and the sled dog teams delivered. But years later, after World War II, airplanes and snowmobiles started replacing sled dog teams. But there was one man who didn't want the tradition to end: Joe Redington, Sr."

His thoughts veered again. *I'd like to start a tradition with Sophie: rolling on a bearskin rug beside the fireplace; sinking into her warmth during each long, dark Alaskan night; making her scream my name each time she comes.*

"When did the race begin?"

The softness in her voice made him grow harder. *Concentrate on the story, not your cock, dude.* "March of 1973. He started the race to save both the history of sled dog teams and the Alaskan huskies themselves, like Sleigh Belle here. They weren't being bred anymore since snowmobiles were faster. Redington also wanted to preserve the historic Iditarod trail. Almost a thousand dogs leave Anchorage in the race: Each team starts with around sixteen dogs. Along the trail, they have twenty-six or so checkpoints they have to make. The record finish was just under nine hours, but the crowds cheer until the last team crosses the finish line; and just like our military doesn't leave a man behind, the race doesn't leave a dog behind. They have something called the Red Lantern Award. They light a lantern at race time and let it burn until it's presented to the last team in, no matter how long it takes."

"What do the dogs eat out there?" Sophie asked, biting her lower lip.

Concentrate on the dogs, not on her moist, full, kissable lips. "The dogs get enough kibble to give them about ten or twelve thousand calories a day, and the mushers—that's the drivers like Grace—supplement the kibble with fish and other sources of high fat. Unlike us, the dogs can run for hours and not deplete their fat reserves."

"Are they all as friendly as these guys?" Sophie asked.

Not as friendly as I want to get with you.

***

Jesus, I wish he'd get friendly with me. I'm about to ignite here. Sophie begged for the Iditarod lesson to end so they could get on to a real race: one to prove who could make the other come first.

233

Cole continued. "Sled dogs are very affectionate. They kind of don't have a choice—they're around humans all the time. They love to stand on their back legs and drape their paws over your shoulders for a hug."

Sophie rubbed her shoulders, wishing Cole would drape his body across hers.

"They love to run and crave being hooked up to a sled and going to work."

I'm craving being hooked up and going to work with you: long, passionate bouts of work.

"They often howl in unison, like a choir...."

I'm going to start howling if you don't stop talking and start touching me.

"They love to run," Cole continued. "And it's a good thing they're used to the harsh temperatures—Grace says the temps are comfortable for them. She also taught me that only a few types of dogs meet the requirements to race. The first are Alaskan malamutes, which have thick coats and incredible endurance. Their faces tend to be white and framed with brown hair, and they have long noses. Next are mixed breed Alaskan huskies like Sleigh Belle. She and her siblings are the ultimate racing machines; well, at least her siblings are. They're descended from a few other hearty breeds, like the German shorthaired pointers, Anatolian shepherds, and Salukis, with some wolf breeding thrown in for good measure. Rounding out the mix are Siberian huskies, which Grace says are about the friendliest of the lot. And strong."

As strong as you when you finally pound into my body? She tried to get her mind focused on the conversation, but it was as hard as climbing a mountain with two broken legs.

"Do they ever race any other kinds of dogs?" Sophie asked, trying to slow down the spinning in her head. "Like, I don't know, German Shepherds?"

"Not anymore," Cole laughed and scratched his emerging five-o'clock shadow which intensified the contours on his face as well as Sophie's lust-o-meter. "But a guy entered poodles one year."

"No, he didn't!" Sophie gasped. "The poor darlings would freeze!"

Cole laughed and put his hand on her shoulder. She went still.

When he withdrew it, she felt cool air surround her again, but it couldn't compete with the heat generated from his brief touch.

"Needless to say, it didn't go well for the poodles," Cole said. "They didn't have the natural fur and undercoat necessary to keep them safe and warm during the race, so that was ended years ago. The race competition is between man—or woman—and animal and nature. Each musher feels he or she has the best tactic for winning: a special menu for the dogs, running in the day versus night, or pursuing different training schedules. But they all run under the same rules: their dogs must have food and boots to protect them from the hard shards of ice, and the musher must have food as well as an arctic parka, an ice ax—"

"And snowshoes?"

"That's right, and a good sleeping bag."

We'd only need one sleeping bag, mister sexy. Our bodies would generate all the heat we'd need.

Cole reached out and placed his hand on her thigh, making Sophie's voice catch.

"So, who's the leader?" Sophie asked. "The musher or the dogs? I bet it's these guys." She ruffled the hair around Sleigh Belle's neck.

"No one dog is the star. They work better as a team than most humans. You have a lead dog, like Zeus, but even the wheel dogs—the ones that help steer the sled— are important, as is the musher. The dogs are ultimately his, or her, responsibility. Their lives are in the musher's hands, and sometimes, the musher's life is in their paws."

"Wow," Sophie said, her eyes wide with wonder. She felt herself sliding deeper under his spell. The staid businessman had been replaced with a man who was relaxing in a barn and stroking a sleeping puppy. She yearned for him to ditch the history lesson and take her into his arms, kissing her until the sun slipped behind the last mountain range. Then she'd beg him to wrap her in his embrace and lower her to the sweet-smelling hay at their feet where he'd spread a thick quilt over the straw, then lower himself over her, making sweet love to her for the rest of the winter.

"Soph, are you okay? You look a little, I don't know...flushed." He reached for her forehead, placing the back of his fingers against her warm skin.

Sophie shook at his tender touch. "I'm fine, Cole. It's just...." She fought to keep the words from coming, from begging him to take her, but she fought a losing battle. "Do you think we could give this—whatever it is—between us a shot?" She reached up and ran her fingers along the side of his cheek.

Cole leaned into her touch. "Soph, I want you. God, I want you so much. But I can't. I...."

She let out a slight moan as he cradled her head, then she closed her eyes.

"Look at me, Soph."

She did as he asked, deciding to take one last chance. "Please?"

Closing his eyes, Cole let out a deep breath. When he opened them again, the turmoil she'd seen reflected in them before had shifted to heated desire.

Cole lifted Sleigh Belle from Sophie's lap and gave the pup a nudge toward the other dogs, then cradled Sophie's chin in his hand and leaned in to kiss her.

The last thing she remembered before the rest of the world ceased to exist was thinking how his lips were softer than Sleigh Belle's fur and smoother than the best whiskey she'd ever tasted.

CHAPTER SIX

Between playing with the sled dogs and having the best sex of her life, Sophie felt happier than she had in years. She'd discovered a side of Cole she didn't know existed. Before, he was determined to stick with his plan to facilitate his mother's recovery and then return to his rule-laced, rigid corporate world. But after seeing him interact with the dogs, and in the wake of earthshattering lovemaking with this sexy, caring man, she felt her resolve to give up on men evaporate like snow in the desert. She and Cole were more like kindred spirits than she had imagined, and they'd just broken the cardinal rule of their fake engagement. As he helped her dress after making love, she realized this couldn't be the same irritating man she'd met at Cassandra's wedding.

After locking up at Grace's, Cole took her to the next destination on Lorenzo's list: a local farm where he watched her learn to milk a goat. When she finished milking the last scruffy girl goat at the farm, she wiped her hands on her jeans and glanced at Cole who seemed to be doing nothing but staring at her all afternoon.

"What? Do I have milk on my face?" She wiped her sleeve against her cheek as she tried to remove an invisible drop, knocking off the earmuffs she had purchased during a quick stop to refuel the truck.

Cole chucked, picking up the gray ear covers and replacing them on her head. "No, just taking in all that is Sophie." He ran his fingers down her cheek and then leaned back, crossing one boot over the other. "You, my dear, are a paradox."

"What do you mean?" Sophie felt her insides turn to mush as he perused her with warm, knowing eyes that now knew intimate details about her.

"Just that you're not what I expected. Yet at the same time, you're exactly what I expected."

"That makes no sense," she said.

"Just like you." He laughed and grasped her hand in his. "So what's next on that list of lover boy's?"

Sophie withdrew the paper from her coat pocket and smoothed the sheet with her mittens. "Looks like the Christmas parade."

"Great," Cole huffed. "Just what I always wanted to do: stand out in the cold and watch as other people stand out in the cold, cheering for floats covered in snow that's cold. Can't we go back to Grace's barn and stay warm together?"

"Come on, Scrooge. Let's go see that parade. We'll keep each other warm several times tonight in my hotel room."

Sophie gave the last milked goat a final pat, eliciting a long "baaaaaa" from the contented creature before it resumed chewing on strands of straw.

Heading toward the truck, Sophie felt herself being nudged away from Cole by a very determined goat. "How cute," she said, ruffling the miniature beast's fur. "He's saying hello."

"Rascal's not that civilized," Cole said. "He's staking his territory." He redirected the goat with a swat to its hindquarters. "He's claiming you as his own."

"What do you mean?" Sophie asked, watching as the goat returned between them, once more pushing her away from Cole.

"Growing up on the *Rocking M*, we had goats," Cole said. "Lots of the pint-sized beasts. Turns out, the males are very protective of females—of any species. They would pry me apart from my girlfriends, nudging me away like I was the devil, not letting me near any of them. It sure made finding a place to make out difficult."

Sophie giggled at the thought of this determined man being thwarted by tiny little goats.

"Sure, go ahead and laugh. But you've never been head-butted by one of these guys." He ran his hand through his hair and rubbed his temple. "See this scar?"

Sophie leaned over Rascal to get a closer look. "Geez, that had to have hurt." She rose on her tiptoes, touched the scar as if the wound was still fresh, and kissed the ouch away. The softness of his skin mixed with her scent on him from earlier made her feel more like a woman than she had in years. Having a famous Italian pursue her did nothing for her libido, but this personal moment with Cole stoked the blaze inside her belly that he had started, a blaze that had lain dormant for far too many years.

"It did," Cole said. "Felt like a knife on fire. It was the first and last time I tangled with one of these creatures. They are determined and fierce."

"I'm beginning to believe you," Sophie yelled as she ran around Rascal and tried to get back close to Cole.

But the goat was determined to wedge between them. And wedge between them he did.

"It looks like you're right," she said, giving in to the game, resigned to walking a few feet away from Cole with the goat strutting between them.

"Of course I am," Cole said, winking at her. "I'm always right."

Sophie grinned. "But the question is, are you fast? Race ya!"

***

Cole froze as Sophie's lithe body careened around trees and snowbanks to make it to the truck before him.

It's lust, pure lust. It's not love. It can't be love. You don't do love.

But the word and concept had dominated his thoughts ever since he'd had the most mind-blowing sex ever. He watched her bounce around Rascal, then lunge for the door before the love-stricken billy goat could nestle up to her again. *I know the feeling, bud.*

On the ride back into town, Sophie talked about everything from wanting to adopt Sleigh Belle, to her new-found fear of male goats, to topics closer to home. "Where's the *Rocking M?*"

Cole watched the one stoplight in town turn to green, shifted the truck into gear, and pulled around to pass a portly man driving a snowmobile down the street. "It's not too far from Coral Cove. About a half-hour north."

"How come I didn't know about that?" she questioned. "That you grew up so close to Coral Cove?"

"It's a little dot on the map northeast of Houston that most people pass through and don't realize is there. It's in the county next to Coral Cove, so I went through a different school system. I haven't been back since...since Dad passed away ten years ago."

Sophie watched him like a child watches a mechanical toy, trying to figure out how it works. "Wow. Ten years.

That's a long time. How'd you end up in Arizona at Nicky's company?"

"Nicholas and I met in college—University of Texas—the year after my dad died. He chose the Air Force. I chose his dad's company."

Sophie raised her brows, silently requesting more information.

"I may not be the size of a linebacker, but I'd always worked with my hands and liked to build things. So working for a homebuilder, and more than that—for a man who stepped in when I'd lost my dad, felt like the right decision after college. Mr. Sterling gave me an opportunity I couldn't refuse. I learned the business from the ground up: from construction crews to contractors to the financial side of things. He promoted me to VP of Operations just three days before he passed away. I knew Nicholas would come back to take over the company, but I didn't know he'd leave the Air Force for good. Not until I met Cassandra and saw them together. Then I understood why."

Sophie leaned back against the leather seat and smiled. "I grew up with both Mel and Cass, but for some reason, Mel and I clicked. We're like sisters. I grew up with Jack, too; and man, has he turned into one heck of a grown-up. I knew in high school he and Mel would end up together. And look how that turned out, albeit six years later."

Cole put on his blinker and turned onto a one-lane street. "Nicholas told me about how Jack was a selfish bastard in high school, according to the girls, and how he made an about-face to win Melanie back. Naming his espresso bar in her honor was priceless. *The Double Shot*— what a great name." Cole thought of the sacrifices both Nicholas and Jack had made to win their women. Could he give up who he was to win a woman? To win a woman as different from him as Alaska was from the Arizona desert?

Sophie interrupted his thoughts. "It's like we're on a different planet up here, isn't it? All this snow everywhere?"

Cole turned his head to slip her a grin and patted her jean-clad leg.

She was quiet for a few minutes, watching the scenery pass by, then skootched to her side of the cab and crossed her arms. "Do you think there's anything we have in common besides a love for peanut butter? Anything at all?"

"I'd say we're pretty good in bed together." He arched his brows and sent her a sexy grin. "But other than that, I doubt it." He turned back to watch the road.

"What's your favorite color?" Sophie asked.

"Blue."

"Darn. Mine's pink."

"That's a newsflash," Cole said, smirking at her and nodding at her passion pink nail polish.

"Fine. Make fun of my color choice. How about your favorite movie?"

"Casablanca," he shot back. "What about you?"

Sophie smiled. "Beauty and the Beast."

"Why that one?" Cole asked.

"Because they were such opposites, yet their love bridged every obstacle put in their way. Do you like quiche?"

"Nope."

"Seriously? How about wine?"

"I'm a scotch guy."

"Favorite snack?"

"Chocolate peanut butter macaroons."

"No kidding? That's mine, too! We have a winner! I knew we'd find something we had in common."

"Don't forget the sex," he added, sending her a wink.

Sophie smiled wide. "So what's your favorite thing to do at Christmas?"

Cole's smile took a quick downward turn, shifting into a frown. "I don't celebrate Christmas."

"What?" she asked, cocking her head and staring at him as if he had sprouted antennae and was talking to an alien race. "Everyone celebrates Christmas. It's the most wonderful time of the year, and all that."

"Not me. I don't do Christmas."

"How can you *not* do Christmas?"

Cole was quiet for a few moments, then decided he didn't have anything to lose by telling her a portion of the truth.

"My dad died on Christmas Eve."

Memories from the worst day of his life played like a movie in his head, crushing his heart into shards as much now as ten years ago. How could he have failed his father when he needed him most? How could he have been so selfish?

Silence filled the cab as Sophie blinked her surprise. "Oh, Cole, I'm so sorry. I guess I can see how that would take all the cheer out of it for you. It's always been my favorite time of the year. All the kids singing Christmas carols, the fancy decorations, the 'reason for the season.' But if my dad had passed away on Christmas Eve, I guess I wouldn't feel like celebrating either."

"Do you have any traditions?" Cole asked, eager to force the past back into the past and not ruin the holiday for Sophie.

"Do I have traditions?" she said. "You bet your cute ass I have traditions."

Cole turned to face her and grinned. "So you think I have a cute ass?"

"I know you do, big fella," she said, patting his thigh that flexed at her touch. "But back to my traditions...." She turned to face the road and sat up higher in the seat.

"First is decorating my house with every piece of garland and string of colored lights I can find. Then I go out into the woods behind my house and cut down the best Charlie Brown Christmas tree I can find, you know—the scrawniest one—along with the thickest, bushiest one I can hunt down. Then I get out all my favorite ornaments and hang them on the two trees while playing every Christmas CD I own. After that, I paint my nails in alternating red and green."

Cole laughed.

"*Shh.* Sometimes I paint polka-dots on them for ornaments. To top it all off, on Christmas Eve, Mel and I have a bake-a-thon and make our famous chocolate peanut butter macaroons. Then she helps me shoot mistletoe down from a tree out back, and we hang a sprig of it near my fireplace."

"Why?" Cole asked.

Sophie lowered her head and fiddled with her fingers. "Because it's magic."

"It is?" Cole asked.

"To me it is," she whispered. Her breath fogged lightly on the window.

Cole reached over and took her hand.

"Anyways, after that, Mel and Cass and I, and now Nicky and Jack, will meet at *Decadent Desserts*—Mel and Cass's chocolate shop—to whip up dozens of macaroons, drown ourselves in vats of eggnog, sing Christmas carols, and toast the season with lots of bubbly. Since Jack connected Mel's shop to *The Double Shot* recently, I'm guessing we'll exchange gifts on Christmas Eve there again this year and add in a few spiked espressos."

"Sounds nice," Cole said, shaking away a sudden shot of envy he hadn't expected to feel. He realized he wanted to be part of their celebration. Part of her celebration.

"Then on Christmas day, I drive over to my parent's place in San Antonio, and we eat the biggest meal of the year: tofu turkey, green bean casserole with all those yummy crispy onion thingies, candied sweet potatoes, cranberry sauce, dressing, and the best sweet potato cobbler this side of the Mississippi."

Cole couldn't speak. It sounded like she lived for the holiday he hadn't been able to bring himself to celebrate for an entire decade.

"Cole? What's up?"

He shifted the truck into park and pointed ahead. "We're here."

CHAPTER SEVEN

Christmas songs blared from speakers on floats making their way down the single snow-dusted street spanning the length of Hardly. The Veterans of Foreign Wars rode in a yellow antique trolley with their VFW logo painted on the side. Behind them was the bread delivery truck from the next town over. After that came dancing women from the new aerobics studio that had opened in the fall.

Bordering the festivities were the townsfolk, dressed in heavy overcoats, thick boots, and some with knit masks covering their faces. Several rubbed their arms and jogged in place, trying to keep warm in the five-below wind chill weather, but most of the natives seemed acclimatized to the cold.

"I don't see a float representing a hair salon," Sophie said, laughing. "Maybe Lorenzo and I should open one here." She squeezed Cole's arm, feeling his muscles clench when she mentioned Lorenzo's name.

"What is it with that guy that makes you fawn all over him?" Cole's jealousy made Sophie feel like a vixen.

"I don't fawn," she said, giving him a friendly swat to his rock-hard bicep. "I tricked him into thinking we were engaged, didn't I? You aren't still jealous, are you?"

Cole stared at the straggly high school band as the handful of students belted out *Jingle Bells* in front of them.

"No. And no, I don't think there's a hair salon in town," Cole said. "The other day, I saw a lady with a grocery bag over her head at the library. I'm guessing it was a bad hair day."

Sophie snickered at his attempt at humor. "Good one, Cole. You actually made a joke."

"Don't get too used to it," he said, shoving his hands into his pockets. "Would you really think about moving up here, away from Coral Cove, and opening a salon with him?"

"Nope, I was just kidding," Sophie said. "I'm too much of a Texan. But sounds like Lorenzo might. The thought had just flitted through my mind." In truth it had streaked into her thoughts like a dark bird of prey when she thought of going back to Coral Cove and having to leave without Cole. She shifted and rubbed her mittens together, then leaned against him and smiled at the mental image of her arms and legs wrapped around his solid naked body when they got back to the hotel, a fire blazing in the fireplace behind them, the heat of his body mating with hers.

Shaking her head, she tried to focus on the crowd in front of them. "I could transform the women of this town, you know. See that lady over there?"

"Which one?" Cole stretched his neck to peer around the horse-drawn wagon with Santa tossing candy to kids as they ran beside him. A grape Jolly Rancher landed on Cole's boot. He lowered himself to grab the piece of hard candy. "I didn't know they still made these."

"I like the pineapple-flavored ones," Sophie said, waving away his offer for the purple piece.

Cole unwrapped the candy and popped it into his mouth. "Which lady were you talking about before the candy-wagon passed by?"

"The one with the straight red hair over there." Sophie pointed between a group of horses and mules that lumbered along. "I could give her a perm that would make that lumberjack next to her drag her off to make sweet love in the barn until next spring." The memory of Cole riding her that afternoon made her panties go damp again. She shifted her legs and couldn't help but brace herself against Cole. It was as if she needed his body heat like she needed oxygen to breathe.

Cole nestled her in his arms, wrapping her in his warmth. "What about that lady over there with the big maroon bow in her hair?"

Sophie sighed. "Hmm. She needs a few highlights and a good trim. Then that big mass of muscle next to her wouldn't be here watching a parade. He'd have her at home, unwrapping her under the tree."

Cole gathered her close, planting a kiss on top of her head. "Do you have sex on the brain now?"

"It's that crazy goat," Sophie said, snuggling into his embrace. "Rascal got me to thinking of you as a man."

"Just the goat?" Cole questioned. "No other reason?"

Sophie giggled and bent her neck back so she could look up at him. "What do you think, big boy?" She winked at him, then lowered her head so she could watch the bugler, proud in his World War II uniform, belt out revile. "But ever since I met you at Nicky and Cass's wedding, I assumed you were a boring, up-tight, regimented, by-the-rules kind of guy. Definitely not someone I'd ever be interested in, even though our one kiss did momentarily confuse me."

Cole raised one brow. "And now?"

"Now I think I could be persuaded to be more than a fake couple if you're interested in breaking a few more rules." She wiggled her hips against him, then swatted him on the ass and dashed out to join the group of seniors dressed up in red coats, green leggings, and tinsel-laden tutus, shimmying their hips to a catchy rendition of *All I Want for Christmas is You*.

***

Cole rubbed his jeans, wondering if he'd ever get tired of watching Sophie do things he didn't expect—like cartwheeling down the road in the middle of an Alaskan Christmas parade.

"That's a helluva gal you've got there," a gravelly voice said from behind him.

Cole looked to his left and saw Buddy, the barkeep from *The Purple Moose*, approach.

"The other night she said she was your fiancée. S'that so?"

"Looks that way," Cole said. He watched as Sophie flitted from one child to another, swinging them around in a circle before giving each of them a hug. Hardly wasn't a big town, not that two-hundred and fifty people was unusual for a place in Alaska. And it looked like Sophie was giving them each an extra heaping helping of Texas holiday spirit.

"Well, you've got your hands full there, my friend." He slapped Cole on the back.

"Buddy, you talk to lots of people in the bar. Do you think people can change who they are?"

"What do you mean?" he asked. "Like change their personality? Their likes and dislikes?"

Cole was quiet, then spoke over the cacophony of the six-member middle school band marching by. "Change what they've thought they wanted their whole adult lives. Forgive themselves for things they did in the past."

Buddy turned from the out-of-tune band to face Cole. "She's gotten to ya, hasn't she?"

Cole watched as Sophie took the scarf from her neck and wrapped it around an elderly woman in a wheelchair across the street. "Yeah. She has."

"Well, my advice to you is figure out why you think you want what you've always wanted: Is it a reaction to something that's happened in your past, or is it truly who you want to be? Most of the time, I've found it's a reaction. Most people don't have the balls to get it together and live the life they want to live instead of wandering aimlessly through the one that's dictated by circumstances they couldn't control in their childhoods."

Cole mulled over Buddy's assessment. His dad's death had been the biggest factor in his decision to move away from the *Rocking M*, away from his mother. Too many memories crowded in his head: All the good times they'd had as a family, the smell of his mother's lasagna wafting through the halls of their sprawling ranch home, the guilt of letting his dad down. He couldn't handle seeing the house, the fields, the animals without yearning to have his dad back.

But after leaving Sterling to care for his mother, he'd realized he not only missed being around his mom—he also missed spending time with his brother and his nephews and nieces.

Searching the crowd for Sophie, he spotted her dancing with a ninety-year-old man gripping a cane, and if the smile exposing his dentures was any measure, he was having the time of his life. Cole felt himself being drawn to Sophie's essence, to her zest for life. He yearned to be the one dancing with her.

"I'll give it some thought," Cole said. "Thanks, man."

"Anytime," Buddy said. "Just make sure you don't let the things that happened in your past screw up your future. Don't keep it bottled up. It ain't scotch."

Cole looked at him, puzzled.

"Only store up the good memories. That's what scotch in a bottle is." Buddy shook Cole's hand, then slapped him on the back and departed for *The Purple Moose*.

Cole reminisced about his teen years and the choices he'd made. Was he strong enough to confront them? But there was a bigger question: Would he be strong enough to overcome them? Feeling an internal drive he hadn't felt for years, he found himself determined enough to push past the fiancé ruse and see if there was something real with the intense, almost electrical connection he felt with Sophie. Maybe she could help him heal; work his way past his guilt. She almost had him wanting to celebrate Christmas again, wishing he could unwrap her under the tree and hold her in his arms forever.

CHAPTER EIGHT

Sophie searched for Cole as she ran against the push of the parade crowd, like a salmon swimming upstream. Finally, she spotted his Stetson towering above the citizens of Hardly.

"Cole! Come quick!"

Cole grabbed her arms and steadied her so she wouldn't trip over the curb. "What is it, Soph?"

"It's Lorenzo," she said, out of breath from running.

"What's lover boy gone and done now?" Cole asked, pursing his lips and planting his hands on his hips.

"It's not actually Lorenzo." Sophie had to stop talking for a second. She bent over to catch her breath, then looked up at Cole, worry etched on her face. "He called. He said he's been trying to call, but he couldn't get through until now. Your mom—she fell, and he can't get her to wake up."

"What?" He grabbed her hand and dragged her along behind him. "Come on!"

Sophie's breath was forcing air from the deepest crevices of her lungs. "You go start the truck. I'll be right behind you."

"I knew I shouldn't have left her," Cole spat out. "I never should have spent the day away from the house. She wanted to do too much by herself." Cole threw open the driver's door, shoved the key in the ignition, then grumbled when she hoisted herself into the passenger seat. "Christ, we were having sex when she needed me." He stepped on the gas and skidded on a patch of ice behind *The Purple Moose*. "Did Lorenzo call 9-1-1?"

She shifted in her seat and embarrassment enveloped her face, her cheeks turning bright red. "He didn't think about 9-1-1."

"Shit," Cole spat out. "What kind of an idiot is he?"

"He's from Italy." She linked her fingers together and tried to steady them in her lap. "He says he's not very good in emergencies."

Cole looked up, glaring at the snowflakes daring to fall. "Why did Mom have to move way up here to the edge of existence? Why did she have to fall? Why is my life so screwed up?" He hit the steering wheel with the edge of his fist. Once, then twice.

Sophie laid a hand on his thigh. "You're not screwed up. You're a loving son who likes things to go according to his plan. Let's see how we can fix this. I'll call 9-1-1." She grabbed her phone from the dash and tapped out the numbers, praying for someone to answer. "Dang. I can't get through." She stared at the display. "There's no signal out here."

"I hate this wretched place," Cole growled. "The closest ambulance is two hours away. I checked into that when I came up to take care of her. Why did she move way out here all alone? At her age?"

"She's not that old; she just has bad luck with falls."

Twenty minutes later, Cole shoved the gearshift into park and opened the door to a gentle snowfall. His boots crunched the snow as he leapt from the truck, then took the front steps two by two.

Sophie sprinted behind him, thankful her boots from the general store were holding up. She had taken inventory of the town and realized Hardly didn't even have a police or fire station.

They needed help.

Cole's curses boomed as he skidded across the floor to his mom. He felt for her pulse and laid his cheek against her mouth to feel if she was breathing.

Lorenzo reached up toward Sophie. "Oh, my sugar cookie, I tried to get Miss Marilyn to sit still. I told her I could make the next round of cocoa. When she slipped and hit her head on the counter, I leapt to her rescue. She is making noises but is not conscious. I ran on top of my shoelace and tripped. I think my ankle bone is cracked." He pointed to a knot the size of an orange on his ankle, his eyes rolling back into his head as he fainted, his head crashing against the sink cabinet.

"Lorenzo!" Sophie screamed, reaching for him.

"Sophie!" Cole snapped. "She's alive, thank God. Run to the bathroom and grab her medicine bottles— there are three of them. We've got to get her to the hospital." He glanced toward Lorenzo, then added, "Both of them to the hospital."

She reached for a throw pillow in a basket near the sofa and placed Lorenzo's head on it. Springing to her feet, she hurried to do as Cole requested. "How far is it?"

"Far enough we probably won't be driving back tonight."

"I refuse to stay behind." Lorenzo's Italian accent broke through as he raised a finger. "I can handle a broken bone. See?" He ran his finger over the knot once more, then his eyes rolled back as he fainted again.

Cole lifted his mother, strode out the door, and carried her to the truck.

Sophie laid out blankets and cushions to make the ride as comfortable as possible for her. She prayed Marilyn would wake up and start discussing the latest in hairstyles and new shades of nail polish she'd found in magazines from the general store.

Cole ran back inside to hoist Lorenzo over his shoulder, but the Italian was too heavy for him. "Wake up, you doofus."

Lorenzo was groggy, but he didn't like being called names. "Who do you call this 'doofus'?"

"You, you big oaf," Cole ground out. "You're going to have to help walk outside. I can't carry you."

"I can walk on my own," Lorenzo said, taking a step and screeching like a bobcat. "Okay, maybe I need a little bit of help."

Cole and Lorenzo clambered outside, gripping each other's shoulders, until they got him into the front seat of the truck where Lorenzo promptly passed out again.

"That dude passes out more than anyone I've ever met." Cole secured Lorenzo's seatbelt, then sprinted to the driver's side. "Soph, can you sit in the back with my mom?"

"Of course." She climbed up into the back seat and laid Marilyn's head on her lap. After making sure Marilyn was secure and warm, she checked her pulse every ten minutes during the two-hour ride to the hospital.

***

Cole cursed himself for not having been with his mother when she needed him the most. *How could you choose to be with Sophie over you own mother? How could you, after what happened with Dad? Shit, when will you ever learn?*

Skidding on a patch of ice beside the emergency room entrance, Cole slammed the gearshift into park and flung open his door. He sprinted around the truck and ran into a petite nurse with a pixie haircut poking out from underneath her blue cap. Cole begged her to take good care of his mother. Fear and frustration lodged in his throat, making his words emerge more like pleas.

Hospital attendants wheeled two stretchers out and loaded up Marilyn and Lorenzo, admitting them to the emergency room.

Sophie held out her hands to Cole. "Give me the keys. I'll park the truck." She tilted her head toward the emergency room's sliding glass doors. "You go on in with them."

"Thanks," he said, dropping the set into her hand. Turning toward the hospital he hesitated, lifted his head, and prayed out loud: "Please let her be okay. I can't lose her, too."

Cole hated the scent of antiseptic mixed with pain and grief. Bad memories from the last time he'd been in a hospital flooded his mind as the hands on the black and white institutional clock overhead ticked off seconds; then minutes; then hours. At four o'clock in the morning, a doctor entered the waiting room, asking for the family of Mrs. Masterson.

Cole rose and covered the distance between his chair and the doctor in two strides. "How is she?"

Sophie stepped up behind Cole, letting him talk with the doc.

The doctor extended his hand and shook Cole's, then Sophie's. "I'm Doctor Evans. Your mother is going to be fine. She has a slight concussion, so we'll need to keep her here under observation for a day or two."

"Then I'll be here," Cole said. "As long as she is."

The doctor nodded. "She'll make a full recovery. As for her companion...."

"He's not her *companion*." Cole spat out the words, then jerked his head toward Sophie. "He's hers."

"Wait a minute," Sophie interjected. "Lorenzo is not my companion. I'm *your* fiancée, remember?"

The doctor smiled as he watched the couple spar. "Regardless, he has a broken ankle and will need to be on bed rest for at least a week."

"And who's going to take care of him?" Cole asked.

Sophie let out a deep breath. "I guess that's going to be me."

The doctor chimed in. "Mr. Romano should be released within the hour."

Cole nodded, then turned to Sophie. "After I can see Mom, I'm going to drive you and lover boy back to the hotel. Then I'm grabbing her some clothes and essentials to make her stay more comfortable."

Sophie glanced out the window and saw the snow drifting down like cottonwood in July, silhouetted against the beams of light from the parking lot. "The snowfall isn't heavy yet, so you should be able to get back up here before it gets too bad."

"Good," Cole said, the sharpness and distance apparent in his voice.

Sophie froze. He'd just dismissed her from his life. Her heart clenched tight in her chest at the change in Cole's attitude toward her. He was discarding her like he'd swipe a piece of lint from his custom-tailored business suits. There was no way she could compete with his mother...and no way she wanted to. "Let's get Lorenzo and head back to Hardly."

"Would you like to see your mother and soon-to-be-mother-in-law before you go?" The doctor looked back and forth from Sophie to Cole. "She's been asking for you both."

"Of course," Cole said.

Sophie nodded, not trusting herself to speak without begging Cole to want her to be there with him; begging her to stay with him for better or for worse.

"Good," the doctor said. "It'll lift her spirits. She's in One-Oh-Four, down the hall. Just make sure not to tire her—limit the first visit to ten minutes, tops."

"Will do," Cole said, thanking Doctor Evans and shaking his hand before the elderly man left to make his rounds.

Cole ran his fingers through his hair and then covered his mouth with both hands, running them down the dark shadow of scruff that had appeared on his cheeks during the past few hours. "Let's go in."

Sophie took a step back and shook her head. "I can't do this anymore, Cole."

"What do you mean, you can't do this anymore?" he said. "Can't do what?"

"I can't lie to her anymore."

"You're picking a fine time to get all moral and ethical on me. Just suck it up and play your part. It'll make her happy."

Sophie swallowed the hurt he hurled at her in the tone of his voice. She cringed at the coldness of his words, yet witnessing how devoted he was to the one person on earth he loved, she couldn't help but fall even further for him. She knew they came from two different worlds: she was grits, and he was caviar. A relationship with him would have the same chance of working as one between a python and a badger. One of them would squeeze the life out of the other. Regrets would fester and grow, eventually squeezing between them like a jealous goat. There were simply too many differences in who they were, what they wanted out of life.

"I'll do it just this once," she said. "Then we're telling her the truth. I can't pretend with her anymore— she might die believing a lie."

CHAPTER NINE

Cole skidded over ice-covered roads, swerving to avoid a moose here, a caribou there. When he slammed on his brakes to veer away from a tree that might or might not have been in the middle of the road, Sophie splayed both her hands on her window and gasped. "Stop!" she screamed, banging on the glass.

"My dearest apple blossom, what is the matter?" Lorenzo asked, stretching out in the back seat, tracing the edge of his cast with a finger, then fidgeting with his crutches.

"I have to save her!" Sophie screamed.

"Save who?" Cole craned his neck to look out the window.

"Bambi!"

"Bambi?"

"Yes, Bambi!" Sophie forced the door open, and took off, stumbling through the snow, yelling across the vast quilt of white, a thicket of dark trees outlined in the distance.

Lorenzo's voice trailed after her. "Come back, my little butter biscuit!"

Cole's nerves snapped and he glared at Lorenzo. "Stop calling her those ridiculous names!"

Lorenzo glared right back at him, anchoring his hands on his hips. "I am fighting for my woman. Much more than you seem to be doing, mister fancy pants."

"Don't call me fancy pants, lover boy."

Sophie glanced back at them, then shook her head, garnering stares from the dueling suitors.

She turned toward the forest and waved her hands as she screamed: "Run, Bambi! Run!"

Ahead of her, a deer raised its head from a basket of what must have been bait because a hunter in camo with a raised rifle waved his hands at Sophie, shooing her away.

"Run, Bambi! Run as fast as you can! He's going to kill you!"

The Sitka black-tailed deer stared at her doe-eyed, its muscles emerging as they tightened, then it leapt across the snow as gracefully as a gazelle and disappeared into a tuft of alder bushes.

The hunter looked at Sophie with murderous eyes and sent her the international sign for "shove it" before disappearing into the woods.

Sophie's heart hammered in her chest as she stopped running. She huffed and puffed, trying to catch her breath. The air felt like it was forming ice crystals in her lungs, making little spikes of pain poke through her chest. *I need to start working out. And I need my coat on—why can't I remember I'm in Alaska?* She bent over and placed her hands on her knees, then lifted her head and flung her middle finger toward the hunter. "That's right, you Bambi killer! Run! Run far, far away!" She stomped her foot, then heard the tiniest clinking sound, like ice when you pour a warm drink over it. The crackling became louder and she felt the earth shift under her feet.

What the– She felt herself falling, then cold water closed in around her, echoing as it filled her ears and burned her skin.

She fought to rise to the surface, panic and adrenaline infiltrating every nerve, every artery in her body. She flung her arms above her head and kicked her feet, fighting to rise to the surface. She broke through to suck in a breath of air, then felt herself descending back into the dark depths. The water was so cold that she couldn't open her eyes. Her lungs burned as she held her last breath, not wanting water to fill them up. But in the frigid liquid, after what felt like a lifetime of struggling to the surface again and again for gulps of air, her limbs wouldn't cooperate. Within moments, she felt her arms start to relax over her head, and the world began slowing down around her.

"What the hell?" Cole jerked open the door.

Lorenzo sputtered gibberish as his long hair hung by his ears, his curls droopy.

"Call 9-1-1! Now!" Cole grabbed his coat, then ran as fast as he could, sprinting toward the place he last saw Sophie before she disappeared underneath the ice-covered lake. *Please don't die, Soph! Please hang on!*

Two hands splashed in front of him, flailing in the water. He slowed as little as possible, careful not to break the ice beneath him. Kneeling, he crawled out onto the frozen lake, stopping just short of the jagged edge that marked where Sophie had fallen in.

Reaching his hand into the freezing water, he grabbed for the wrist closest to him. A finger slid over his palm before it slipped under the ice cold water and out of his reach.

Leaning forward as far as he could without falling in, he plunged his hand under the water and jerked as the coldness made the breath hitch in his chest. Running his hand back and forth, he felt slippery skin against his. Taking the chance, he lowered his hand two more inches below her wrist, then gave her arm a death grip and pulled up as hard as he could.

His mind's eye created non-stop scenarios of what might happen: Sophie emerging with full-fledged hypothermia, slipping out of his grip, or worse—dragging her up from an icy grave, already dead. He couldn't tell, given how numb his arm felt.

The jagged edge of the ice hurt like hell, slicing his forearm and wrist, but he dragged Sophie's thin wisp of a body up and over the edge of the ice.

She wore a thin pair of crimson leggings, one red boot, and a now see-thru long-sleeved *Be Kind to Animals* t-shirt that at any other time would have made him vote her the winner of a wet t-shirt contest. But right now, he'd settle for her being alive.

He rubbed his hands hard down her arms and wrapped her in his thick coat. He hugged her close, got his footing, and readied himself to lift her into his arms. But he stopped, realizing their combined weight might break more ice. "I'm sorry, Soph. I'll try to make this as quick as possible." He slowly backed away from the hole in the ice, dragging her behind him for a few feet until he felt the frozen lake could hold them both. Gathering her in his arms, he ran full speed back to the truck.

"Can you hear me?" He screamed louder than he wanted at her, but he was terrified he'd been too late. Her body lay blue and lifeless in his arms.

He clutched her body to him like a mama bear does with her cubs. Breathing hard against her neck, he tried to warm her cold body.

"Please hang in there!" he begged. "Don't die on me, Soph!"

Lorenzo hobbled on his crutches to the truck's back door and opened it for Cole. "Mister Alaska, I cannot get a call to go through. No bars will leap into my phone."

Lorenzo reached for Sophie's hand, then dropped it like it was covered in spikes and threw his hands over his mouth. "Is she...*dead*?" He began to wail, then flung a hand across his head and tilted it back as he began singing what sounded like an accented version of an old time religion hymn.

"Grab the blankets from the back seat!" Cole shouted.

"Yes, of course," Lorenzo said, halting his song and gazing at Sophie.

"Run, you idiot!"

"Oh, yes! Lorenzo runs for his cherry popsicle!" He tottered toward the truck, grabbed two thick blankets, and stared at Cole. "Oh, that was a bad name, was it not? Very inappropriate. Oh, I must apologize."

"Don't just stand there! Lay a blanket on the ground!"

Lorenzo propped his crutches against the truck and braced himself. He turned to flick the blanket in the air, and it drifted down to cover the snow.

Cole laid Sophie's cold body down and felt for her faint pulse. Then he placed his cheek next to her mouth. *Shit. No breath.*

"Come on, baby." He propped her head back a couple of inches, pinched her nose, then breathed two deep breaths into her mouth. He pressed his hands together and started chest compressions. "Cover her up with the other blanket, you moron!"

Lorenzo settled the second blanket over Sophie and began reciting a litany of prayers.

After administering two more breaths, Cole began compressions again, then he heard water erupt from her lungs.

She sputtered and jerked, then coughed up more water.

Cole placed his hands beneath her neck. "Sophie? Can you hear me?"

Her small voice crackled and hitched. "Did s-she g-get a-away?"

"What? Did who get away?"

"Bambi. D-did she g-get away?"

Sophie's innocent blue eyes stared up at him, begging him to say what she wanted to hear.

Lorenzo knelt down and grabbed her hand. "Yes, my apple strudel, you saved the deer! You are a hero!"

"What the hell?" Cole snarled. "You almost drowned in an ice-cold Alaskan lake, and you're worried about a damn deer?"

Sophie smiled, then closed her eyes and settled back into a contented sleep.

CHAPTER TEN

"Oh, my sugar plum, you are alive! Grazie to the heavens!" Lorenzo drug his cast behind him and settled onto a three-legged wooden stool beside Sophie, brushing away a few strands of hair still stuck to her face. "We almost lost you, my gingersnap. Then what would happen to my heart?" He bent down to kiss her hand, then caressed it like it was a cherished heirloom.

"Oh, please," Cole said in his deep baritone. He felt he did nothing but roll his eyes whenever the Italian spoke.

Sophie smiled at Lorenzo. As he bent down to kiss her, she turned her head away to expose her cheek instead.

Cole saw her face flush as she spotted him staring at her.

"Cole."

"Sophie. Nice of you not to die on us."

"I did my best, seeing as I mean so much to you." She pulled a yellow patchwork quilt up under her chin and held her hands there as she looked around the dark wooden room. A fire crackled in a brick fireplace by her feet, and a dim oil lamp flickered on an old farmhouse table, the light playing on antique glass windowpanes. "Where are we?"

Cole approached the army cot he had laid her on, pulled up another stool, and stroked her hand. "We're in an old hunter's cabin. Lorenzo couldn't get 9-1-1 on the phone—big surprise there—and after I got you breathing again, you passed out. Since you fell in that lake, a full-fledged blizzard has settled in, so we had to find some sort of shelter and a way to warm you up if you were going to have any chance at all."

Without a doubt, he'd switch places with her if it were humanly possible and be the one almost freezing to death. He'd do anything to get her warm again, to save her.

He glanced at Sophie and realized she had slipped into slumber again. She looked peaceful, like a baby falling asleep after a long bout of crying.

Watching her doze, he tried to imagine what life would be like without her, without her carefree and caring spontaneity. She had awakened a will in him: a will to live life for her and for himself, to see the world in more than black and white. For the first time since his dad's death, he viewed life in Technicolor again. She had given him that gift. He felt himself falling for this quirky, selfless, vibrant, deer-saving woman. His life seemed boring and dull compared to the one she experienced on a minute by minute basis.

But that same spontaneous lifestyle had almost cost his mother her life. If he hadn't been traipsing around the Alaskan wilderness with Sophie, making sweet love to her perfect body, he could have kept his mom from taking her latest fall and ending up with a concussion. No—his way was the right way of living for him, the responsible way. Duty trumped fun. Always had—since his Dad's death. Always would. Always should.

Lorenzo pulled his stool closer to the cot and began rubbing Sophie's feet through the quilt. "You're a very lucky man, Cole."

Cole turned toward him and looked puzzled. "Why?"

"Because the angel laying before us loves you more than anything in the world."

Cole turned to look at Sophie, his heart clenching in his chest. Could his feelings be love, too?

"I may be a flaky hairdresser to you, but I talk to numerous women in my line of work, and I've learned quite a few things about 'em. And what these eyes see layin' in front of us here is a woman who loves you more than she loves her free spirit. She loves you more than a pig loves wallowing in slop."

"Slop?" Cole turned to look at Lorenzo. "What happened to your accent?"

Lorenzo grinned and raised his shoulders, holding out his hands. "This is my real accent. I'm from a tiny town in south Georgia. But in my profession, it pays to sound exotic." He grinned, then held out his hand toward Cole. "My real name is Larry Roberts. Pleased to meet ya."

Cole let loose a hearty laugh and shook the man's hand. "You, sir, should be an actor. You've got Oscar-worthy material there."

"That's the point, isn't it?" Lorenzo withdrew his hand from Cole's and placed it back in his lap. "And before you say anything else, I know all 'bout your pretendin' to be engaged to Sophie."

"How'd you know?" Cole questioned.

Lorenzo glared at him. "Oh, please. You two are so obvious. I knew it from the moment she threw herself all over you at *The Purple Moose*. It was fun to play along: makes life interestin', you know? But now—after what happened to Sophie—you must tell her how you feel. You have to tell her before it's too late."

"Look Lorenzo. I mean, Larry...."

"Lorenzo's fine. I'm used to it."

"I do care for Sophie. Very much. But with my past...." He rubbed his hands across his face. "Even without that, we're too different. Her fall in the lake made me realize I can't live with her kind of spontaneity."

Lorenzo rose and patted him on the back. "My friend, the question is, are you sure you can live without it?"

***

"I'm so c-c-cold." Sophie fought to get the words out before her shivering made speech impossible.

Cole gathered more blankets around her, like he was tucking in a toddler. "Is that better?"

"Not really, but I ap-p-preciate the effort." She attempted to smile at him, but her face was still too cold and stiff to do much more than open her eyes.

Cole swept strands of hair away from her face, exposing the bloody cuts on his arm.

"Wh-h-at's that on y-your arm?" she asked, concern in her gaze.

Cole turned it toward the firelight. "Just some blood. That ice was pretty sharp."

"Oh, my gracious. Blood?" Lorenzo, back in character, looked at Cole's arm, then crumpled onto the floor.

"Seriously? You're going to pass out again?" Cole grabbed a blanket from a trunk in the corner of the one-room cabin and covered Lorenzo's body with it, tucking a few layers of the thick fabric underneath his head. "If recent history is any gauge, he'll be out for at least an hour now."

"Could you p-please come lay beside me, Cole? I'm s-s-so c-c-cold. I c-c-can't seem to get warm."

Cole hesitated, then unbuttoned his shirt and crawled beside her under the quilt. Pulling her into his arms, he tugged at the fabric of the t-shirt—his t-shirt—she had slipped into during one of her brief periods of being awake.

"Mind if I take this off?" he whispered. "Just so that you can warm up faster. Direct body heat warms a lot quicker than through a shirt."

Sophie nodded and allowed him to remove the t-shirt. He wrapped her in his arms, pulling his flannel shirt around her, enveloping both of them in the fabric that still held his warmth.

She felt her intense coldness begin to dissipate as his body heat made its way through her skin, or maybe it was the attraction to him she felt heating her from the inside. How easy it would be to get lost in his protective warmth for the rest of her life.

As the minutes ticked by, she felt her insides stirring. She knew the skin-to-skin was life-saving—not sexual—but she could feel his cock react to their closeness, the smoothness of their skin touching, the scent of their attraction.

Cole drew a finger down her cheek, then stroked his warm hand along her side and gently massaged the top of her thigh.

Sophie relished in the feel of his caresses, even though she knew his goal was checking her body temperature.

A half-hour later, she must have warmed enough for him to feel like he could roll out from under the quilt without endangering her recovery.

Sophie's eyes opened at the separation, feeling the cold leap back into her core.

Catching the reflection of the flames in his eyes, she watched as he leaned over to kiss her. And at that moment, she wanted nothing more than all of him: his tender kisses, his caring heart, his unspoken love. Nothing in the world could stop the draw she had to feel the soft skin of his lips pressed against hers this one last time.

Sophie had never been so happy, so content. She drifted back to the safety of sleep where she lay in the warm embrace of her knight in shining armor. She couldn't imagine being anywhere else in the world.

A dream...it's just a dream.

Her knight swept her away: Took care of her every need and made sweet, passionate love to her.

Please be real...Pretty please.

But she knew it could never be. Not for more than this one time. Her dreams had been filled with images of them together, making love like it was their last time, melting into each other's arms, becoming one. She knew the images were now dreams she would relish for the rest of her life.

Then the dream transformed into a nightmare: Freezing water surrounded her as she looked up to see heart-wrenching fear on the knight's face as he fought to rescue her from the life-draining water.

Once again, her spontaneity had caused more problems than good. This time, it had almost killed her—and him. Halfway between sleep and wakefulness, she shivered at the flashback of slipping deeper into the frigid water, feeling her body begin to slow down—to shut down—and grasping at the single lifeline she had: the knight's strong hand—Cole's hand.

She'd almost died. That changed a person. She didn't regret saving the deer's life, but acting before thinking couldn't be in her future. Not anymore. She had to be more conservative and careful. Like her knight. Like Cole.

In her mind, she explored different scenarios, ones that wouldn't have endangered her life, or Cole's, as her dream gave way to wakefulness. She could have screamed at the hunter from the road. She could have reached over and honked the horn to distract the deer. Anything but running full speed onto a frozen lake without thinking of how dangerous it could be to her. Or to Cole.

That was it. Sophie decided the future must be different. Starting now. Or at least, starting when she could keep her eyes open.

CHAPTER ELEVEN

The door braced against the onslaught of snow, but Cole knew he had to find some food for the three of them. The sun's late-morning rays glistened in deep oranges across the white blanket the blizzard had left behind, covering everything as far as he could see.

How am I going to find any food in this mess?

His stomach grumbled at the thought of a juicy steak, then quelled as he imagined how Sophie would disapprove.

Strawberries...think about delicious, sweet strawberries. As sweet as Sophie's....

After tossing and turning on the cold, wooden floor during the early morning hours, he'd decided sleep was futile, so he took an inventory of everything else in the cabin: a stack of firewood in the corner, a second oil lamp on the opposite windowsill, a pair of snowshoes hung above the fireplace, and a bowl and pitcher placed atop a small table in the back corner. Besides two stools, the cot Sophie rested on, and the pillow and quilt that came with it, the cabin didn't offer much else. He'd opened the cabinet doors on a wardrobe by the front door, hoping to find some cans of food, but all he found were a few dead spiders left over from the summer.

Lorenzo snored like a bear beside the smoldering embers while Sophie slept as quietly as a mouse. Cole walked around the cot and reached up for the snowshoes.

Fear and frustration washed over him. What if he couldn't find anything to eat? Or worse, couldn't find help? He didn't have the slightest idea where they were, nor if there was a human in existence for miles. But he knew one thing for sure: he couldn't let Sophie down. He had to save her, even if he died trying.

"What are you doing?" Sophie's soft voice broke the stillness of the dawn.

"Time to go find us some food, sweetheart," Cole said. "There isn't a bite to eat in this whole place."

Sophie shifted to her elbows and looked out the window. "Wow, that's a lot of snow out there."

"You're telling me," he said, trying to figure out how to latch the snowshoes so they wouldn't come off.

"Cole?"

"Yes?"

Sophie sniffed a couple of times, then raised a corner of the quilt to rub her nose and turned her head toward him. "I'm so sorry I ran out on that ice. You could have died."

"Me? You're the one who fell in."

"I know," she said. "But sometime in the middle of the night, I realized I was being selfish, only thinking of me and how good it would feel to save that deer. I didn't stop to think about how it might affect you. That you could have been hurt. If something had happened to you, I would never have been able to forgive myself."

"It's okay, Soph," Cole said, reaching over to stroke her cheek. "Everything's turned out fine. Except we need some food now."

"Is there anything I can do?" she asked.

"I'll put some more logs on the fire," he said. "Just keep lover boy here company until I get back." He cocked his head toward Lorenzo and his incessant snoring.

Sophie smiled at him. "Will do. And Cole, we should tell him and your mom the truth as soon as we can. We shouldn't be lying to anyone anymore. Life's too short."

"Don't worry about that just yet," Cole said, shrugging into his coat. "We'll figure out the best time to drop the bomb on them." He turned and began pushing against the door. "The sooner I can get us some food, the sooner we can figure out how to get out of here."

Sophie nodded. "Be careful out there."

"I will. Be careful in here." He glanced toward Lorenzo and chuckled. "I have a feeling you'll be just fine."

Sophie awoke to the sound of dogs barking and yipping. A double knock echoed off the door as it opened and brought a whoosh of arctic air inside. The sound of voices wove its way through the one-room cabin.

"Sophie, how are you doing, girl?" Grace barged through the door with a backpack slung over her shoulder. "We've all been so worried!"

Behind her came Cole, a victory smile spanning his face. "I brought the cavalry."

Grace laughed deep and hearty like Santa. "The dogs and I found him out picking berries off the few bushes not buried in snow."

Sophie looked to Cole, then back at Grace.

"He refused to catch a rabbit for food," Grace boasted. "Said you were a vegetarian and you wouldn't touch it even if he did."

Cole laughed and handed Sophie a bowl full of berries. "That's right, sugar plum. Veggies and fruits headline the menu for you."

Lorenzo laughed. "Hey, you're using my lines there, mountain man."

"Damn straight," Cole said, tossing an apple to him.

Just then, a whirring noise from above the cabin crescendoed, growling louder and fiercer by the second, as though it planned on grinding the roof off.

"What's that?" Sophie asked, hunkering down under her quilt.

"The rest of the cavalry," Cole said, grinning like he knew a state secret.

Grace shifted on the stool next to Sophie. "The grapevine works quicker than a party line up here, thanks to two-way radios. Cell coverage is shitty, so we do it the old-fashioned way. Anyways, Doc Evans is my uncle. He radioed when Cole didn't make it back to the hospital last night. He said Marilyn was frantic and wouldn't stay in her bed, even tried to talk a candy-striper into letting her borrow her car. So Doc called Buddy."

Grace turned to glare at Cole. "If you'd just told my son about your mom, he could have flown her to the hospital in his helicopter." She softened her gaze and looked back at Sophie. "That's what you're hearing right now, sweetie."

Voices became louder as Sophie heard boots stomping on the front stoop, ridding them of snow before entering the small cabin.

"My dear, are you alright?" Marilyn marched in and took up residence on the second stool. "I heard all about your tumble into the lake." She leaned close to Sophie, gentleness coating her words. "Are you feeling okay? Do you need some hot cocoa?"

"Oh, Mrs. Masterson...."

"I'll have none of that 'Mrs. Masterson' crap. You're going to be my daughter-in-law. Call me Marilyn."

Sophie's face went pale as she caught Cole grinning at her from his perch in the corner.

"But you don't know about—"

"Of course I do," she whispered. "I know all about you and Cole trying to fool me. But if there's one thing that can't be pretended, it's true love. And that's what I see between you two."

"Now everyone, let me take a look at this young lady." Doc Evans stepped around the cot and pulled his stethoscope out of his leather case, shooing everyone out into the cold for a few minutes. He mercifully warmed the instrument a long moment before the fire, then listened to Sophie's lungs and heart rate. After a quick exam, he proclaimed her to be healthy and safe and the crew was allowed back in.

"Howdy folks." Buddy swung open the door, letting in another brisk wave of cool air. Shutting the door behind him, he dug into his jacket and handed Cole a small box. "I think this is what you were lookin' for, man."

Cole took the package and tucked it into his coat pocket. "Thanks, Buddy. I owe you one. Technically, I owe you my first born, seeing as how you brought your chopper all the way up here to help us out."

"That's what we do in Alaska, my man; help each other out. No rules. No excuses."

CHAPTER TWELVE

After loading up with the others in the helicopter, Cole waved to Grace as the chopper lifted into the sky.

Grace sent him a snappy salute, then mushed her sled dog team back toward her house.

Buddy flew the bird like he was part hawk, banking around Marilyn's backyard before executing a perfect landing like the National Guard pilot he was.

Lorenzo escorted Marilyn out of the chopper as Cole scooped Sophie into his arms.

"You okay, there?" Cole asked.

Sophie smiled up at him. "Never better," she said. But her smile lit up his world for only a brief second before worry creased her brow. She whispered, "We still need to come clean with Lorenzo since your mom already figured it out."

"In due time," Cole said, sending her a wink. "Maybe later today."

"Okay. Just so long as we're honest with him."

Cole bent down so he could give her a quick kiss, then with deep strides in the snow made his way to the house.

Lorenzo had shoveled most of the snow from the steps, not complaining once about the inconvenience of his crutches or having to use his insured hands for the task. He had even laid out logs in the fireplace and started a fire.

Cole looked back and waved to Buddy as the helicopter lifted into the sky to fly Doc Evans back to the hospital. He sent them a quick salute before climbing the stairs to the house. Grateful to be back in the small abode, he laid Sophie on the sofa in the family room next to the fireplace and drew a blanket up to her chin. "I want you to keep warm. You've been through quite an ordeal."

Marilyn fawned over Sophie, bringing her hot drinks and preparing her a parade of vegetable dishes to eat, topped off with various berries and fruits for dessert.

"Thank you all for being so wonderful and for helping me," Sophie said, setting down the porcelain cup on the coffee table beside her. "But I have to apologize. I've ruined everyone's Christmas."

"Are you kidding?" Marilyn said. "There hasn't been this much excitement around here since the female moose decided to drop her calves in my backyard. We're just so thrilled you're okay."

"Here, here, my little cinnamon dumpling."

"Lorenzo—" Cole knew Sophie was starting to tell him everything had been a lie.

Lorenzo waved his hand at her. "Not now, my butterscotch pudding. I want to savor this moment with my new friends and give thanks for all my blessings this Christmas Eve."

"Oh, my," Sophie said. "It's Christmas Eve. I almost forgot."

Cole knelt by the sofa and pulled her into his arms. "Time to get you into bed, or Santa might not come visit tonight."

Sophie wrapped her arms around his warm neck and gave him a squeeze.

His whole life had been turned upside down in the matter of a few days, and he didn't know if he could make it right again. He'd fallen in love with his total opposite and wasn't sure he could win her over.

Cole smiled down at Sophie as he lowered her onto his bed like she was a precious, rare blooming flower. He drew the thick bedcovers up and tucked them under her chin, then whispered, "Be sure to make a Christmas wish before you fall asleep."

She nestled her head into the soft pillow and gazed up into his eyes. "Even if I know it won't come true?"

Cole kissed her forehead, then tapped the bridge of her nose lightly with his finger. "Especially if you know it won't come true."

***

Sleigh bells interrupted Sophie's recurring dream starring her seductive and brave knight. A gentle hand rubbed across her forearm, awakening her from her slumber.

"Wake up, sleepyhead. It's Christmas." Cole knelt next to the bed and smiled at her. His hair was mussed from sleep, making him look sexy and tempting.

"Merry Christmas, Cole." She shifted in the bed and scooted back until she was sitting up. "You have a very comfortable bed. Where did you sleep?"

"I took the sofa," he said. "Glad you like my bed. Maybe we can share it one day soon." He waggled his eyebrows.

Sophie's cheeks blushed at the thought, hoping maybe her Christmas wish might come true after all.

As seemed to be the norm since her fall into the lake, Cole scooped her into his arms. She took the opportunity to breathe in his scent, the warmth of his masculine skin mixed with homemade soap, as though it were her last time to make a memory of him.

"Merry Christmas!" Voices surrounded them as Cole carried her into the family room.

"But what.... How—"

Melanie ran to hug her best friend as Cole situated Sophie on the sofa. "Girlfriend, you scared us all! But your personal Santa made sure since you couldn't come to Coral Cove for Christmas, he brought your Texas Christmas to you!"

Jack walked over and enveloped Sophie in his arms. "Merry Christmas, you crazy girl. No one but you could get into such a quagmire, and we all love you for it."

Cassandra and Nicholas approached next, wrapping Sophie in a group hug. "We love you, Sophie. And we are all *so* glad you made it through such a harrowing ordeal."

"There's no way I could have survived if it weren't for Cole." Sophie reached for his hand and squeezed it. Facing death had changed everything. She wouldn't take the happy moments in life for granted any longer.

Nicholas slapped his friend on the back. "He's one in a million. I'm hoping I can persuade him to come back to Sterling now that Marilyn's on the mend."

"Before this week, I might have said yes." Cole looked at Sophie and smiled. "But now, I think other plans might be stepping in to take up my time."

Sophie cocked her head and looked up into Cole's golden eyes. "What do you mean?"

Lorenzo burst into the conversation. "It means, my little toaster strudel, that mister fancy pants is in lo-o-ove. And I couldn't be happier for you both." He smiled at Sophie, then slapped Cole on the back.

"Lorenzo—" Sophie started to talk, but Cole stopped her.

"We have a Christmas understanding," he whispered.

Lorenzo sent her a wink. "Yes. It seems I have a new apple dumpling," he said, crossing the room and enveloping Marilyn in his arms. "Santa brought me a sweet gift this year that I didn't expect."

Lorenzo shared the secret details of his identity with everyone as well as his excitement about his budding romance with Marilyn and his decision to open the next *Romano's Salon* in Hardly.

"Here, here!" Cole said, raising a glass of orange juice to the new couple in their midst. "To Larry and Mom!"

"Let's add some champagne to that and make this a real celebration," Marilyn said, grinning like a schoolgirl with her first crush.

Sophie sat up on the sofa, surrounded by the people she loved and scanned the room that had been transformed with an array of very familiar Christmas decorations.

"Hey, where did all this come from?" she asked, pointing to the two trees flanking the fireplace. "And the ornaments—"

Melanie scooted closer to Sophie and draped her arm over her shoulder. "Cole called us all last night and explained everything. Nicky and Cass flew out to Coral Cove and we loaded up his plane with your Christmas ornaments and decorations."

"You called them? You made all this happen?" Sophie looked at Cole who shrugged his shoulders.

"I wanted to make this the best Christmas ever for you," he said.

"But the trees? How did you know?" She looked at the two trees: one fluffy and full, the other scrawny and barren, save a few dangling ornaments.

"I'm a good listener." Cole smiled at her. "I remembered you telling me about your traditions. I wanted to make sure you had both your trees on Christmas morning. Trees are one thing they have in abundance around here, that's for sure."

"Time to eat," Marilyn announced from the kitchenette.

Cole strode over to the stove. "What've we got?"

"Pancakes with fresh blueberries, courtesy of the Texas gang, pure maple syrup, boysenberry syrup for those of you who want an extra kick, orange juice, apple juice, grits, hash browns, toast, and a side of chocolate peanut butter macaroons."

"Those are mine!" Sophie and Cole said at the same time.

The room erupted in laughter. Nicholas spoke up. "Now I *know* you two are meant for each other. No other couple on the planet would eat chocolate peanut butter macaroons for Christmas breakfast."

Sophie stuffed a macaroon in her mouth, savoring the smooth sweetness of the peanut buttercream frosting mixed with the crunch of the chocolate-flavored almond cookies surrounding it.

After several rounds of mimosa toasts and multiple helpings of pancakes, Cole stood, cleared his throat, and tapped a spoon against the side of his juice glass. The room quieted as all eyes focused on him.

"All the craziness aside, I have an announcement to make." Cole walked toward the sofa and knelt down in front of Sophie. He took her hands in his, raising each to place a gentle kiss on them. "You, Sophie, have helped me realize that lightening up doesn't mean changing who I am, but I've realized I've been living my life on autopilot—ever since Dad died."

"Oh, dear," Marilyn said, bringing a hand up to cover her mouth.

"It's okay, Mom," Cole said, then turned to address his friends and family. "I've never told anyone my secret, but it's time to take responsibility for my actions. The day Dad died—ten years to the day yesterday—I was supposed to be helping him with the round-up. Instead, I'd snuck away with my girlfriend. She was leaving for

Colorado the next day with her family and we wanted to be together one last time." He faced his mom and continued. "If I had been helping Dad like I was supposed to, maybe he would have survived the heart attack. Maybe I could have gotten him to the hospital in time."

"Oh, Cole," Marilyn said. "Have you been carrying around this guilt, this feeling of responsibility all these years? Is that why you won't date anyone for very long?"

"Mom, I'm so sorry." His voice caught on the words he finally could say.

"Cole, I don't need to do this, but I feel you need to hear it: I forgive you. Your dad forgives you. Please, live your life. Your dad and I had many wonderful, perfect years together, but God had other plans for him."

Cole reached to hug his mother, wiping away tears that were years in the making. "Thanks, Mom. I think I needed your forgiveness. And Dad's."

He turned to Sophie and took her hands in his. "I didn't want to care for anyone anymore because I was terrified of not being there when they needed me. I couldn't survive if the people I loved got hurt because of me. But when I saw you disappear under that lake, the hurt of realizing I might not ever be able to tell you what you mean to me—how you've transformed my life—all of a sudden seemed more important than holding onto the guilt. At that moment, I felt I was the one dying. At that moment, I realized that living without you would be worse than any fate I could imagine."

A tear crept past Sophie's lashes. Cole reached up, wiping it away with tenderness. "Sophie, a very smart man—Lorenzo, in fact—made me realize that each crazy, erratic, spontaneous decision you create makes my life so much better. He said I should let Sophie be Sophie, and not try to change you. He is so right, because if I changed you, you wouldn't be the woman I've fallen in love with."

Sophie fell forward into his arms and hugged him with all her might.

Cole held her tight, kissed her soundly, then rocked back on his heels. "I have three Christmas presents for you that I'd like to share in front of everyone. First is an announcement." He turned toward Nicholas. "My best friend on the planet, Nicholas Sterling, has been so gracious as to offer me my job back when I am ready. Thank you so much, Nick." He nodded toward Nicholas, then turned to face Sophie again. "But I've made another decision; one that feels right. I'm going to go back to Texas and try and make a go of it at the *Rocking M*."

"Oh, Cole," Marilyn said.

"And I'd love for you to come back if you'd like, whenever you'd like, Mom. But it's going to be different from the ranch you and Dad created, because I want

Sophie to be happy there. It's not going to be a cattle ranch anymore. It's going to be an animal rescue shelter and a vegetable farm. I'm going vegetarian."

Sophie squealed like a kid covered in a pile of Christmas gifts and leapt into Cole's arms.

"And in honor of Sophie," Cole continued, hugging her tightly, "I'm taking Jack's example and renaming it the '*Frolicking S*.'"

Everyone looked at each other in total silence, then Nicholas tossed his head back and howled. "You are *so* smitten, my friend. Mister meat-eater-turned-vegetarian—I've seen everything now! To the *Frolicking S!*"

"Here, here!" Everyone toasted each other, clinking their mimosas and glasses of juice together as Sophie wiped away tears.

Cole raised his drink again, tapped it with a spoon, then disappeared into the bathroom. Poking his head around the door, he said, "Ready for your next gift, Sophie? Does anyone hear sleigh bells?"

Sophie nodded and wrapped her arms around her waist as everyone turned to see what was making the racket behind the door.

"Merry Christmas, Soph!"

Barks filled the air as Sleigh Belle rounded the corner and leapt straight into Sophie's arms.

"Oh, Cole! It's Sleigh Belle! Hi there, girl!" She hugged the puppy and reached out her chin for the wet kisses the husky showered her with.

"She's adorable," Melanie said. "I love her Christmas collar." A red band of ribbon covered with green bows and golden bells circled Sleigh Belle's neck. Each time the husky puppy barked, the bells jingled.

"Cole, thank you so much!"

"You're welcome, Soph. And now for my third gift."

"Wait a second. This has to be perfect," Melanie said, scrambling to her feet and grabbing a sprig of mistletoe from her purse, attaching it to the lamp that curled over Sophie's head.

Cole shook his head, not understanding what mistletoe had to do with his third gift. "Sophie, you've changed my life. It's like I was living in a black and white world before I met you. Now it's filled with vibrant color and changing patterns I never could have imagined. You've turned it into a real life." He paused for a moment, then continued. "Soph, I love that you are such a free spirit. I love that you travel to Alaska with more nail and hair products than winter clothes. I love that you make my world a happier, more colorful one. I love that you smile all the time." He sank his hand deep into his pocket and withdrew the package she'd seen Buddy hand him at the cabin. "I love you, Soph. You have opened my heart and made it live again." He revealed the contents of the box, and Sophie clasped her hands over her mouth.

"Gracious, Cole. It's stunning!" She picked up the sterling silver necklace with two intertwined hearts outlined in small diamonds.

"Buddy's a jeweler, too," Cole said. "This is his latest creation."

"I love it, and I love you." Sophie traced the edges of the hearts with her finger, then leaned over and kissed Cole on lips that tasted better than a dozen chocolate peanut butter macaroons.

Melanie looked confused, but Sophie smiled to reassure her it was okay. She didn't need the magic of mistletoe. She had something better.

Sleigh Belle nestled into Sophie's lap as Cole took the necklace from her hands and fastened the clasp behind her neck. "I love you, too, Soph. And I promise I will always be there for you." He kissed her like a groom kisses his bride, the whoops and hollers from their audience fading into the distance behind them. When he pried himself away, he grinned. "Now, let's open the rest of the presents."

EPILOGUE

Six Days Later

"Cole, come have one of Jack's new drinks." Sophie sipped from a demitasse cup, then curled her index finger, beckoning him over to *The Double Shot's* antique bar.

"I'll be there in a second," he said. "Just have to get Sleigh Belle's collar fixed. She and Charlie got tangled up in the bushes again, but at least they're settling down in their beds by the fire now. I think they like each other."

Sophie approached him and bent down to pat each pup on the head. "They're sweet, aren't they?"

"Not as sweet as you, my sugar cookie."

"Stop that," Sophie said, laughing as she stood back up. "That's Lorenzo's line."

Cole leaned in to kiss her cheek. "Whatever you say, my blueberry tart."

Sophie swatted his arm, then sank into his embrace, savoring the feel of his hard body against hers. Tuxedos always made a man look fabulous, but the feel of the soft fabric covering Cole's solid frame was a turn-on she hadn't expected.

The day after Christmas, Nicholas had flown the Coral Covers back to Texas in time to prepare for their traditional New Year's Eve bash, along with Sleigh Belle and all of Sophie's decorations. Lorenzo and Marilyn joined them for the trip, determined to explore the attraction blossoming between them in a warmer climate.

Music and laughter filled *The Double Shot* and *Decadent Desserts*. Coral Cove had seen quite a year: Cassandra and Nicholas's marriage, Melanie and Jack's engagement, and now Sophie and Cole's growing love.

Betty and Addie waddled over and tapped Cole on the shoulder. "Mind if we cut in, young man? We need a word with Sophie."

"Not at all," Cole said. "I'll go grab a drink with the guys. Just make sure she's available for me before the clock strikes midnight." He winked at the women as they enveloped Sophie in a group hug.

"Of course," Betty said, turning her attention back to Sophie. "We're so glad you're back from Alaska in one piece and that you've found such a wonderful, not to mention handsome, young man."

Addie patted Sophie's back. "And thank you, dear, for bringing Lorenzo Romano to Coral Cove. Betty here just about fainted when she saw him glide through the front door with those luscious curls of his."

Betty's cheeks turned bright red, prompting her to fan herself with a box of Melanie and Cassandra's chocolates she'd lifted from the counter. "Addie, you know Ed and I are courting now. I only want to meet the famous Lorenzo Romano, not marry him." She turned back toward Sophie. "We're dying to consult with him on our hairstyles."

"Not that we don't trust you, Sophie," Addie said, fingering her blue-gray locks. "Just to get a second opinion, you know."

"Would you like me to introduce you?" Sophie asked.

"Would we ever!" the women said together, clasping their hands, their eyes twinkling and sparkling like the lights on the Christmas tree beside them.

"Lorenzo?" Sophie called out across the room, motioning for him to join her.

He wove his way through the guests and encircled Sophie in his arms, then placed a kiss on her cheek. "Yes, my sugar plum?"

"Oh, my." The elderly ladies sighed.

"May we get a kiss, too?" Addie asked, giggling like a school girl.

"But of course, my lotus blossom." Lorenzo placed his hands on their shoulders, then gave each woman a hug and a kiss on both cheeks.

"Now don't you go kissin' on my filly," Ed Peterson, Jack's great uncle, said as he approached the group.

"And Addie's mine now," Ralph Johnson, Ed's marine buddy, said, grabbing Addie's hand. "But we don't mind meetin' someone famous, do we, Ed?" He turned toward Lorenzo and shook his hand. "Pleased to meet ya, mister famous hairdresser."

"The pleasure is all mine. But you and Mr. Peterson are the celebrities here." Lorenzo stood at attention and respectfully reached out his hand. "Thank you for your service, gentlemen. I understand you are two of the reasons we still have the freedom to celebrate occasions like this in America."

Sophie smiled, glad to see everyone she cared about happy and thankful. "You've made their whole year, Lorenzo."

"Au contraire, my peach parfait. They have made mine." He glanced back and forth between the smitten ladies and their men, then turned to listen to their thoughts on the latest hairstyles and military tactics.

Marilyn laughed as she approached the group and slid her hand into Lorenzo's.

Sophie whispered to Marilyn. "I'm so glad you've found each other. He really is a doll."

"Don't I know it," Marilyn said. "And I'm so thrilled you and Cole are together. You're good for him, Sophie. Very good. I haven't seen him this happy since he was a kid."

Cassandra and Melanie joined Sophie and glanced toward the trio of men across the room.

"Can you believe our luck, ladies?" Cassandra said. "Who knew that in the course of one year, we'd all find our happily-ever-after's, and that they'd be here in Coral Cove, laughing and cutting up like brothers?"

They watched Cole, Nicholas and Jack toast one another, then turn and walk toward them.

"Lordy, that's a lot of good-looking testosterone coming this way," Sophie said.

"You got that right, sister," Melanie sighed.

"Makes a girl go weak at the knees, seeing all that manliness and knowing it's ours," Cassandra whispered.

"Glad to be back?" Cole asked Sophie, stepping in beside her, treating her to a seductive smile accompanied by a pre-midnight kiss.

"Mmm...glad to be with you," she said, reaching her hand up to his smooth, clean-shaven cheek. "I must say, I got used to your scruff in the wild north. I wouldn't be opposed to you growing it back occasionally. For old times' sake."

"Anything you wish, my darling," he said. "Would you like a glass of champagne?"

"I think I would. Thanks." She watched as the man she had fallen head over heels in love with strode toward the bar. As soon as Nicholas' plane had landed, Cole's inner Texan began to emerge. And Sophie liked it.

"Hey girl," Melanie said, nudging Sophie with her shoulder. "I meant to tell you; nice dress. Anything you'd like to share with the class?"

Sophie looked down at the red A-frame dress she'd decided to wear for the festivities. Soft pleats started from the jewel-encrusted necklace topping the dress, skimmed her shoulders, then draped down to a finger's-breadth above her knees. Strappy silver stilettos completed her New Year's Eve outfit.

Melanie knew Sophie had hung the dress in her closet several years ago, swearing that when her knight came along, she'd wear it the night he proposed.

"I know it won't happen tonight, Mel, but when I opened my closet, it just seemed right. And besides, it makes me feel pretty."

"You're the prettiest girl in the room," Cole said, sliding a flute of champagne into her hand and a chocolate peanut butter macaroon into her mouth. "No offense, Mel."

"None taken, Cole," Melanie said. "But you'd better take good care of my bestie." She swung her arm around Sophie, then handed her over to her man.

"My pleasure." Cole swept Sophie into a hug and kissed her like a knight in modern day armor.

***

Jack's voice rose above the conversations and festivities filling the room. "Ready to celebrate the New Year everyone?"

Cassandra, Melanie, Nicholas and Jack handed out flutes of champagne to the crowd just in time for the countdown.

"Five, four, three, two, one! Happy New Year!"

Cole pulled Sophie underneath the archway connecting *The Double Shot* and *Decadent Desserts* and gave her a searing kiss, full of love and what she could swear tasted like the promise of a lifetime of happiness. The chocolate peanut butter macaroons he'd fed her earlier mixed with his sensuous kiss, creating a memory that would last in her heart forever. Sophie couldn't imagine being happier. "Happy New Year, Cole."

"Happy New Year, Soph," he said, lowering himself to one knee, then calling out, "Sleigh Belle! Charlie!"

The husky puppy trotted over and sat down next to Cole, dropping a red velvet box bound with a green satin bow into his hand. Charlie waddled behind her with a small gold package in his mouth, then took his place next to Sleigh Belle, wagging his thin tail back and forth beside her.

Sophie knelt down to pet the puppies, then looked at Cole as he took her hands in his.

"Sophie, you are the love of my life; my Technicolor treasure, my effervescent princess, my spontaneous shnookums."

Sophie raised a brow at the last term. "You got help from Lorenzo, didn't you?"

"But of course, my candy confection. But seriously, every day with you is better than all the rest I've ever had combined. I don't understand how I can love you more tomorrow than I already do, but I know I will. And I hope to wake up every morning of my life amazed by how much more I love you than I did when I fell asleep in your arms the night before. Will you please give me the honor of being your husband, of spending every spontaneous day and night with you for the rest of my life?"

"If you don't say yes to that proposal, I will," Lorenzo said, wiping a tear from his eye.

"Yes!" Sophie said, hugging Cole around his neck and kissing him like she was savoring a rare, vintage wine.

Their friends and family laughed, then cheered, surrounding Sophie and Cole with love and support on this night of celebration.

Cole reveled in the warmth and love that was his future. He untied the green ribbon and flipped open the velvet box, removing an aquamarine ring surrounded by a circle of sapphires, emeralds, rubies, turquoise, amethyst, morganite, topaz, tourmaline, and diamonds. "I couldn't bring myself to select a traditional ring. It had to be a reflection of you and all your uniqueness." He slipped the ring on her finger, took her hands in his, then looked into her eyes. "It's perfect."

"You're perfect," Sophie said.

"I've got one more thing to seal the deal." Cole lifted the gold package Charlie had brought over and opened it. Reaching in, he withdrew two chocolate peanut butter macaroons, handing one to Sophie and holding one himself. They linked their arms and fed each other a confection, then sealed the proposal with a kiss.

Melanie lifted her glass of champagne, pointed to the greenery dangling from the archway above the happy couple, and shared the first toast of the new year.

"Here's to mistletoe and macaroons!"

RECIPE

CHOCOLATE PEANUT BUTTER MACAROONS

This is the best macaroon recipe I have ever tasted.
Enjoy these confections with an espresso and
a Coral Cove Romance!

Ingredients:

Chocolate Macaroons:

1 cup powdered sugar

½ cup almond flour

3 tablespoons Hershey's dark chocolate cocoa powder

2 egg whites, room temperature

5 tablespoons sugar

Peanut Butter Buttercream:

½ cup salted butter, room temperature

1 teaspoon pure vanilla extract

1 ½ cups powdered sugar

1 ½ tablespoons whole milk

¼ cup creamy peanut butter

½ cup dark chocolate miniature chocolate chips

Instructions:

Macaroons:

Preheat oven to 350 degrees.

Line two baking sheets with parchment paper.

Have a pastry bag with a plain tip ready.

Blend the powdered sugar, almond flour and cocoa powder together until there are no lumps.

In a separate bowl, beat the egg whites until they hold their shape.

Add the sugar to the egg whites and beat for two minutes until firm.

Fold the dry ingredients into the mixture.

Place batter into the pastry bag.

Pipe the batter onto the baking sheets in one-inch circles, keeping them about one-inch apart.

Rap the baking sheets firmly to flatten the macaroons.

Bake for 15-18 minutes.

Cool macaroons completely before removing from baking sheet.

Buttercream:

Whip butter and vanilla for three minutes or until fluffy.

Add powdered sugar and mix thoroughly.

Pour in milk slowly until it reaches a soft consistency.

Mix in peanut butter and miniature chocolate chips.

Creating Your Masterpieces:

Spread the buttercream mixture on the inside of half of the macaroons after the cookies have completely cooled. Place a second macaroon on top of each to complete the confection.

Best when eaten a day later, after the flavors have had a chance to mingle.

Makes approximately two-dozen Chocolate Peanut Butter Macaroons to enjoy during the holidays. I hope you enjoy the extra crunch the miniature chocolate chips provide. I've always believed you can't have too much chocolate! As Lorenzo would say, "Buon appetito!" And a very Merry Christmas to you and yours!

Macaroon recipe adapted from The Bite-Sized Baker.

ACKNOWLEDGEMENTS

Thanks go first and foremost to my wonderful, supportive, amazing husband, Eric: thank you for always cheering me on, supporting me, and being my number one fan—you are and will always be my true heart's desire. I couldn't do this great adventure without you. Each day with you continues to be better than the last (it's amazing how that's possible!) I love you more than words can say.... Also, many thanks go out to the fabulous group of Stolen Hearts authors who asked me to join them in the initial Valentine project: Hadley Holt, Diane Kelly, Angela Harris, Trinity Blake, and Sherrel Lee—thanks for keeping me on my toes and looking out for my characters—you guys rock! A shout out goes to the "Grammar Guru" and best editor this side of Jupiter, Kevin Gingrich—thanks for challenging me to become a better writer book after book and for making me laugh so hard it hurts. A heartfelt thanks goes out to my writing retreat ladies: Angela C., Amy L., Jana U., Angela H., and Cheryl L.: Cheers, y'all! Also, thanks to the people who have taught me so many interesting things that I was able to incorporate into this series: to my dear mom, whom I miss terribly—thanks for instilling in me a love for baking, for all things chocolate, and for teaching me how to make the best hot chocolate sauce known to man; to Ellen and "Eric the

Brave" for sharing your vast espresso knowledge over the years; to Michelle at the East Bay Starbucks in Charleston for the tutorials on the intricacies of espresso both in drinks and recipes; to Mary and Tom in Alaska for welcoming us into your beautiful (and warm!) home for so many years, for introducing me to dark chocolate (that's for you, Tom!) and for teaching us about your unique state—Alaska truly is the final frontier; to Tony for introducing me to Green, the most beautiful and soft husky I've ever met, and for teaching me about sled dog teams; to Dan for informing me about unique habits of goats and letting me experience it first-hand with his herd; and to Anginette for inspiring the Bambi scene. Happy Holidays!

THE AUTHOR

Cadia Cox reads as many romance novels as she can get her hands on. She loves creating stories and is excited to share *The Coral Cove Series* with you. She is also a photographer and loves to travel, having been to all fifty states and around the world. She loves escaping to the ocean, getting lost in the Smithsonian, discovering new dessert recipes, and, of course, all things chocolate! She lives in Texas with her husband and writes crossover novels under the name M.M. Frische. Please visit her website at www.cadiacox.com.

***

Follow Cadia on Facebook and Twitter:
https://www.facebook.com/cadiacox/
https://twitter.com/CadiaCox

Sign up for Cadia's newsletter at www.cadiacox.com to find out about new book releases and other events.

Also, please check out the list below of "Stolen Valentine novellas—the project that launched C. Coral Cove Series. Visit the authors' websites, read the books, and sign up for their newsletters. Happy reading!

A Sappy Love Story * By Diane Kelly
Hearts, Howls and Heroes * By Trinity Blake
My New Girl Fiend * By Hadley Holt
The Trouble with Larry* By Angela Harris
Stolen Memories * By Sherrel Lee
Heart's Desire * By Cadia Cox

CADIA'S BOOKS

THE CORAL COVE NOVELLA SERIES

HEART'S DESIRE
A Coral Cove Valentine Romance

DOUBLE SHOT OF LOVE
A Coral Cove Halloween Romance

MISTLETOE & MACAROONS
A Coral Cove Christmas Romance

Reviews are like gold to authors.
Please take a moment to leave a review on Amazon for
THE *CORAL COVE SERIES.*
Thank you so much!
~ *Cadia* ~

Look for more Cadia Cox romances to come!

www.cadiacox.com